He swore silently when he couldn't see any enemies. It was as if they blended into the land itself. But he knew they were out there—unless arrows were falling from the sky, which he knew could not be true. He looked over his shoulder, checking the area behind him. He saw no one there either, but that didn't mean some Apaches weren't there, as hidden behind him as they were in front of him.

He lay there sweating, wondering if the Apaches would ever show themselves. He was worried about moving from the spot, unsure whether the enemies were still out there waiting for a better target, or if they had slipped away . . .

Wildgun

End of the Hunt

Jack Hanson

JOVE BOOKS, NEW YORK

This is a work of fiction. Names, characters, places, and incidents are
either the product of the author's imagination or are used fictitiously,
and any resemblance to actual persons, living or dead, business
establishments, events, or locales is entirely coincidental.

END OF THE HUNT

A Jove Book / published by arrangement with
the author

PRINTING HISTORY
Jove edition / January 2001

For information address: The Berkley Publishing Group,
a division of Penguin Putnam Inc.,
375 Hudson Street, New York, New York 10014.

The Penguin Putnam Inc. World Wide Web site address is
http://www.penguinputnam.com

ISBN: 0-515-12998-4

A JOVE BOOK®
Jove Books are published by The Berkley Publishing Group,
a division of Penguin Putnam Inc.,
375 Hudson Street, New York, New York 10014.
JOVE and the "J" design
are trademarks belonging to Penguin Putnam Inc.

PRINTED IN THE UNITED STATES OF AMERICA

10 9 8 7 6 5 4 3 2 1

1

BUFFALO 2 WAS out ahead of Will Barlow and his friend White Bear, as he often was when the two men were taking their sweet time while riding along. The big, shaggy, pitch-black dog seemed completely nonplussed by the snow and the subfreezing temperatures. He just moved along in a zigzag pattern, nose testing first the ground, then the air and back, constantly probing the world in his vicinity. Suddenly the huge Newfoundland stopped, head slightly cocked, as if listening for something.

Barlow, who had seemed to be half asleep, really wasn't. As always, he was alert to everything going on around him. He pulled to a halt. White Bear, having also been aware while not appearing to be, stopped, too. The two sat there, Barlow on his big old mule, White Bear on his Indian pony, their own eyes and ears now examining their environs.

Barlow knew Buffalo 2 was on to something, but whether it was some kind of enemy or simply some carrion that smelled intriguing, he didn't know. He suspected the former, though there was no real reason for that. They were along the well-traveled trail between Santa Fe and Taos, heading to the northern city with some military papers.

They had been in Santa Fe for a few months, and, despite the intimate, lusty attentions of Natividad Santiago and Lupe Nuñez, they were growing bored. With so much time on his hands, Barlow found himself too often thinking of his daughter, Anna. He hated being cooped up in this city for the winter, but knew he had no choice. Still, it was difficult for him because he was certain now that she was in San Diego and he could not yet go to get her. The boredom and the agony of not being able to go to Anna began to get to him, and it was with some relief that he accepted an assignment to take some military dispatches to Taos. White Bear, as bored as Barlow was, had willingly offered to go along.

They were perhaps halfway between the two cities, and were expecting no trouble. The Mexicans had been pretty well pacified since the American army had taken over both places without really firing a shot. And the Indians living in the numerous pueblos in these parts were peaceful all the time, as far as the two visitors knew. But there was just something about the way Buffalo 2 was acting that led Barlow to believe that there was danger about.

"Maybe some bloody Comanches or even bloomin' Apaches are in the vicinity, old chap," White Bear said softly, his words whisked away in the strong wind.

Barlow nodded. It was as likely an explanation as any, and needed no response. His head twisted slowly from side to side on his bull-like neck as he tried to pick up a sound, scent, motion—anything that would give him a clue as to what, or who, was out there.

"Mayhap we ought to mosey on over to them aspens yonder," Barlow whispered, nodding toward a small copse.

"I do believe that would be the bloody prudent thing to do, mate," White Bear agreed.

They moved off slowly, still trying to learn who or what was out there. It was difficult enough, but the strongly blowing wind made it all the more so.

As they moved, Barlow called softly to the dog, who did not respond at first, but then trotted toward the trees where the two men were heading. There, the great dog stood, head again cocked, on the alert once more.

Barlow and White Bear dismounted. While the Shoshoni went to tie off the animals, his companion knelt next to the dog. He rubbed the thick neck. "What's out there, Buffler?" he asked in a whisper. "There some black-hearted ol' hoss or two out there?"

White Bear moved up and squatted on the other side of the Newfoundland. The two men and the dog waited, silent, wary, alert. Minutes passed, then more. Buffalo 2 finally relaxed, and soon began to fidget normally again, seeming like he wanted to be off chasing rabbits.

Barlow glanced at White Bear and shrugged. Both rose. "All right, Buffler," Barlow said, "go on off and do whatever it is you want to do."

The dog bounced off, spraying nearby trees to mark them.

Barlow shook his head. "I know he was on to somethin', hoss," Barlow said.

"I believe you're right, old chap," White Bear replied. "But whatever it was, it seems to have gone off somewhere. Maybe it was just some bloody Mexicans or something riding by over the hill or something."

"Reckon you're right, hoss," Barlow said with a sigh. He looked around, taking in the lowering sun, and the increased chill in the air. "This place looks as good as any fer stayin' the night."

White Bear nodded. It had been his thought, too. He

turned and headed for the animals to unsaddle and tend them. Barlow began gathering firewood. Soon a fire was started and some meat they had brought along was cooking. Coffee was on the flames. The two men sat near the fire, legs stretched out after all day in the saddle.

Buffalo 2 had been roving around, weaving in and out of the widely spaced trees, sometimes bounding off onto the road and its fringes. But now he came over to the two men and flopped down heavily next to Barlow. He still had some flecks of blood on his muzzle, which he licked at.

"Ate well, did ye, boy?" Barlow said with a grin, scratching the big dog's head.

Soon the men were bolting down hunks of deer meat, dripping grease. Finally Barlow leaned back, burped mightily and lit his pipe. "Deer meat may be purty good," he mused aloud, "but I sure do wish we had us some buffler. Goddamn, it seems like a coon's age since I've filled my meatbag with hump meat and ribs."

"You're making me pine for my bloody home, old chap," White Bear said. Though he was smiling, he was serious. It had been a long, long time since he had ridden on the big hunt with his fellow Shoshonis. Not that he minded being here with Barlow, but there were times when he almost wished he were back in his village. Of course, he remembered, at this time of year, the weather would be far worse up north in his country than it was here.

"Hell, if you were home, you'd be gittin' nagged by Bird in the Clouds—if she had even kept you around, hoss," Barlow said. "Plus," he added with a laugh, "you'd be freezin' your balls off in some lodge whilst the wind howled outside."

White Bear laughed. "Hell's bells, old chap, being in a bloody lodge would be more comfortable than sitting here freezing my balls off without bloomin' shelter of any kind."

"Reckon you're right about that, hoss," Barlow said, still chuckling a little.

The two men grew quiet, smoking their pipes, thinking their own thoughts. Night had descended, and finally Barlow said, "Reckon it's robe time fer this chil'." He spread out his otter skin sleeping robe and slid into its comforting cocoon. He was asleep in seconds, as was White Bear nearby in his furry buffalo skins.

A sound filtered through to Barlow, but he was having trouble deciphering it since he was buried deep in the warmth of his sleeping robe. By the time he figured out that Buffalo 2 was trying to warn him of something and he popped his head out into the cold morning, at least half a dozen men were charging into the camp.

Buffalo 2 raced at one who was lunging toward his master, and slammed the man to the ground. He bit the man's face, and then darted toward where another enemy was rapidly closing in on White Bear, who was tangled in his thick robes. The Newfoundland pounced on the man's back, then tore at his flesh, deep growls pouring forth.

Barlow, too, was still partly in his sleeping robes, but he managed to get his hands free, each with a pistol. He fired at one man who was only steps away. The ball slammed into the man's chest, but his momentum kept him going a bit longer and he toppled, landing partly atop Barlow, who clubbed him on the side of the head with the pistol butt, just in case the man wasn't dead yet.

Barlow shoved the body off his legs and scrambled out of the otter robe. As soon as he was on his feet, he dropped the empty pistol and shifted the other to his right hand. He swung toward White Bear, where another enemy was just about to bash his head in with some sort of club.

Barlow fired, and the man went down. "Damn," Barlow muttered as the man rose a moment later, the ball having only winged his arm.

But by now, White Bear was out of his robes and had his war club in hand. He was enraged at the attack, and made more so by his inability for some moments to get free of his sleeping robes. With a mighty chop, he hacked the enemy down. Blood flew, splattering everything nearby, from the man's shattered head.

Barlow spotted two men running through the trees. He bent and scooped up his rifle, dropped to one knee, sighted and fired. One of the fleeing men went down, but the other got away. Moments later, Barlow heard a horse galloping away.

As he rose, Barlow noted that the first man Buffalo 2 had attacked was still alive and was trying to crawl away. Barlow stepped up and kicked the man in the head, and his movement stopped.

"Goddamn, hoss, if that weren't some," Barlow said as a still furious White Bear walked up.

"We're lucky we weren't put under, old chap," White Bear said tightly. The more he thought about being snarled in his robes, unable to get free to defend himself, the angrier he got.

"That's a fact," Barlow said evenly. He could see White Bear's anger, but he felt none of it himself. It had been a close call, but had turned out all right. "I wonder what that was all about," he muttered.

White Bear shrugged, too irritated to say anything.

"Bandits, I reckon," Barlow noted, using his foot to flop the man he had just kicked over onto his back. "That's what they look like."

White Bear nodded and went to stoke up the fire, still trying to let the anger in him settle down.

Barlow went and checked the five bodies. All the attackers were dead. He went back to the fire and gratefully let the warmth float over him. "Three of them boys was Mexicans," he said. "The other two looked like some kind of pueblo Indians. I cain't tell what pueblo they're from. If I was to guess, I'd say they're Taoseños."

White Bear looked up at him in surprise. It wasn't usual for Mexicans and pueblo Indians to fraternize so closely, even in banditry, as far as he had been able to tell since he had been in these lands. "Very odd, old chap," he said evenly. His anger had fled.

"That it is, hoss," Barlow said as he squatted and reached for the coffee. "But I reckon it happens from time to time. Still, it's mighty queersome, and I hope it ain't some kind of harbinger. I've had more'n my share of bad doin's the past couple of years. I sure as hell don't need no more." Especially since he was so close to getting Anna, he thought.

After eating, Barlow and White Bear checked the bodies for anything useful. There wasn't much—a bit of tobacco and maybe ten pesos.

"If these lads were bandits, they were bloody poor ones, old chap," White Bear said dryly.

Barlow nodded. He, too, thought it strange. The weapons the men had were poor. There were only two pistols among them, neither of them looking like it would fire, or would fall apart if it did. There were several knives, dulled from use, and one Spanish-style sword, quite rusted. "Not only that, hoss," he said, "but they was mighty ill-equipped for such an undertaking."

They saddled up and rode out, breath frosting from their noses and mouths. They left the bodies where they were, food for the scavengers. Buffalo 2 took his position out ahead of the two riders, weaving his zigzag trail, nose close to the ground.

Being in no particular hurry, and having seen no sign of other bandits while traveling, they spent another two nights on the trail before riding into Taos under a lightly falling snow. They went straight to the army commandant's headquarters and dropped off the leather satchel full of dispatches. Then they headed for a cantina, hoping to find Rosaria and Inez.

The women weren't there, but the two new arrivals did spot their old friend Manuel Ortega. The Mexican grinned and called them over to his table. As they neared it, the three other men who had been sitting there hurried away.

"*Hola, amigos,*" Ortega said. "I weel buy you a drink?"

"*Muchas gracias,*" Barlow said as he and White Bear nodded enthusiastically.

Moments later, they were sipping harsh whiskey. Barlow and White Bear pulled out their pipes, while Ortega rolled a shuck *cigarillo*. "So, what are you doing back in Taos, *señores*?" he asked.

"Brought some army papers up here from the big chiefs down in Santa Fe." Barlow grinned widely. "And we plumb wanted some robe time with Rosaria and Inez."

"You can't find no women in Santa Fe?" Ortega asked, amused.

"A couple of the finest, but it was time for a change, I reckon."

"You have any trouble on the way here?" Ortega asked, his accent a little less discernible than it had been a couple of months ago.

"That's some odd that you should ask, hoss," Barlow said thoughtfully. "We was attacked by a band of bandits on the trail a couple days ago."

"That's not so strange."

"Maybe not, hoss. But we put five of the six on 'em

under, and three was Mexicans and two was some of pueblo Indians. That strikes me and White Bear as mighty queersome."

Ortega shrugged, suddenly looking highly uncomfortable.

Barlow's eyes narrowed as he glared at Ortega. "You know somethin' about all this, hoss?" he demanded.

"No, *señor*," Ortega said too hastily.

"You've known me a while now, hoss," Barlow said flatly. "And so you know I don't suffer liars well. Now, if you know somethin' about these doin's, you best tell it."

Ortega looked around nervously. He was suddenly frightened, and it showed in his handsome, dark face. "There has been talk, *señores*," he said softly, warily, "between the people of Taos and the Taoseños of . . . revolution."

2

"REVOLUTION?" BARLOW BLURTED out, surprised.

"*¡Silencio!*" Ortega hissed. "*¡Baboso!*—Idiot!" He glanced around the cantina, hoping that no one had overheard. He had nothing against Americans, but many people in Taos—and Santa Fe—did, and if he was heard revealing what was supposed to be a secret, they would have no compunctions about killing him. Fortunately, no one was paying them any attention. He sighed with relief.

"Revolution?" Barlow asked in a whisper.

"*Sí.*" Ortega glanced around again. "Many of the people here are not happy with the arrival of the Americanos," he said quietly.

"You among them?" Barlow asked flatly.

Ortega shrugged. "I still think of this as Mexico, *señor*," he said without apology. "I guess I always will. But the Americanos I have met, they are fine men, mostly. I don't like the soldiers being here, and I'd rather this was still Mexico. But I think it certain that the Americanos are here to stay. I think it's foolish to plot against it." He shrugged again. "I think maybe if the Mexican army came back, I might think differently. But they're so deep into Old Mexico by now that they'll never return."

"You know anything of these plotters' plans, hoss?" Barlow asked after draining his glass.

Ortega shook his head. "I just know there's talk about rising up against the Americanos. I don't think anything will come of it, *amigos*, but sometimes these things get out of hand. I wouldn't be surprised if a few *loco* Taoseños did something foolish."

"Well, I reckon we got nothin' to be concerned over," Barlow said. He refilled his glass and leaned back in his chair. "How you been makin' out, hoss?"

"Bien." He grinned a little. "Life could be better, *amigo*. But, it could be *peor*—worse."

"That's the way it is all the bloody time, old chap," White Bear said.

"Sí," Ortega said rather ruefully. "I'm fine, *señores*," he added. "Running low on pesos. I think I will have to find work soon." He grinned widely.

"Workin'—especially for some other ol' hoss doesn't suit this chil' much neither. I been on my own hook too goddamn long to submit to another man's orders," said Barlow.

"That why you came back here, old chap, when General Kearny ordered you to do so?" White Bear asked with the hint of a smile.

"Them was different times, hoss," Barlow said flatly. He didn't mind White Bear poking a little fun at him, but when it touched close to his search for Anna, it grated his nerves. "That rancid son of a bitch would've shot me down right there."

"I guess he would have at that, mate." White Bear regretted having mentioned it. He knew full well how touchy—and understandably so—Barlow was about his daughter and anything that kept him from finding her. He was a fool to have said such a thing. But to apologize now would only make it worse. So he kept his silence.

Barlow stewed in anger for some minutes, but he finally began to get a handle on his rage. He knew White Bear had meant no harm with his statement. But it still bothered him, and that irritated him even more. Finally he drained his glass and stood. "Well, boys, I aim to go find me Rosaria, if'n I can. You comin', hoss?" he asked, looking at White Bear.

"I do believe I will join you, old chap," White Bear said evenly, rising.

"Adios, amigo," Barlow said, proud of his command of the Spanish phrase. They were among the very few words he knew in that language.

"Hasta luego," Ortega said. As he watched the two walk out of the cantina, Ortega wondered if he had done the right thing in telling them the rumors of revolution.

Barlow and White Bear strolled across the plaza to another cantina. They walked proudly, verging on arrogance.

Barlow was not that tall, though he was a wide, massive block of a man. Long, unruly hair tumbled from a battered, wide-brimmed felt hat and rested on the broad shoulders covered by a simple calico shirt. He still preferred heavily fringed buckskin pants.

White Bear was a bit taller, and much thinner, though still muscular. Pitch-black hair hung almost to his waist. He was still dressed in Taos fashion of wool pants, cloth shirt and short wool jacket, but his bow and quiver hung across his back, and a war club rested at the small of his back, stuck through a rough leather belt.

They entered another dim cantina, glad to be out of the frigid wind. But the two women they sought were not there either. They went from cantina to cantina, most of them off the plaza. In the fourth one, they stayed a while to have something to eat.

"These Mexican eats are plumb tasty," Barlow said as he swallowed another tamale. "But I still declare that buffler's the best."

"I agree, old chap," White Bear said, though he enthusiastically spooned down more of the spicy-hot stew of beans and meat.

Barlow held out a tamale for Buffalo 2, and the animal gulped it down almost whole, barely giving it two quick chews. He sat there, looking eagerly up at Barlow, wanting more. His tail swept the floor.

Finally, full of Mexican food and cheap whiskey, they walked out into the cold again. It was almost dark now, and Barlow was growing annoyed at the lack of success in tracking down Rosaria. Not that he was even sure that she would want to see him. It had been a few months, and a young woman as beautiful, vivacious and lusty as Rosaria could have her pick of the men in town.

Two more cantinas later, Barlow and White Bear spotted Rosaria and Inez. The women were sitting at a table, sipping wine, with several men. Barlow's eyes clouded with anger, and he fought to control it. There was nothing wrong in her enjoying other men; she was not married to him. But it irked him nonetheless.

Inez spotted the two men. She waved enthusiastically, smiled widely, and nudged Rosaria with an elbow.

Rosaria look up and her face brightened, her eyes fairly lighting up the room. "*Mi corazón!*" she yelled. She motioned for the men with her to get out of the way so she and Inez could get to Barlow and White Bear.

The Mexicans, however, were not in a mood to give way to two Americans. One snapped something angrily at Rosaria, and she, in turn, slapped him in the face, anger raging through her.

Buffalo 2 growled as he, Barlow and White Bear neared the table.

The man whom Rosaria had slapped shoved her roughly back into her seat. He reared back to smack her in the face, but a mighty hand grabbed his arm and yanked it back up and around. The Mexican hissed in pain as his shoulder almost separated.

"Ain't nobody ever told you it ain't a manly thing to go around hittin' women, hoss?" Barlow asked quietly, still holding the Mexican's arm in a most uncomfortable position.

The man said nothing, afraid even to breathe lest his shoulder snap in Barlow's powerful grip.

"You boys should be leavin' now," Barlow said evenly. He continued to hold the one man's arm.

The six other men rose cautiously, looking hatefully but warily at Barlow, White Bear and the dog. The latter two moved back a little to give the departing Mexicans a little room.

When the six were past White Bear and Buffalo 2, Barlow shifted his hand a little, increasing the pressure on the man's arm. "Up you go, hoss," he said, easing his grip enough to allow the man to rise. He turned the man then shoved him forward, letting go of his arm. To add impetus, he kicked the man in the backside, propelling him forward into the arms of several of his companions. "*Adios, amigos*," he said with a hard grin.

Barlow turned and smiled warmly at Rosaria, who returned it. Then her face paled, and she pointed, eyes wide.

Before Barlow could turn, someone had smashed a chair across his back, the wood splintering and flying. Barlow grunted, and spun, eyes fiery with rage.

Two of the Mexicans who had been at the table slammed into him, driving him back a step, and bending his torso so his back was on the table, his feet still on the floor.

A knife flashed up in the air, and started to descend, heading toward Barlow's midsection. Then it was gone, swept away by a massive black bundle of teeth and muscle.

The man yelped as the dog's weight and momentum knocked him sideways and down to the floor. A snarling Buffalo 2 gnawed on the man's arm. The knife quickly fell to the floor, but the Newfoundland did not give up. He continued to tear at the man's arm. The man yelled in pain, fear and anger, and tried swatting the dog with his free hand, but the few shots he managed to land were as ineffective as a fly against a buffalo.

As soon as Buffalo 2 had knocked the knife-wielding Mexican away from him, Barlow easily shoved the other man off him, then hammered him square in the face with a mighty fist. The man collapsed in a heap, never uttering a sound.

Barlow stepped on the crumpled Mexican as he headed over to help White Bear, who was managing to keep three men away from him with wild swings of his stone war club. But he could not keep it going forever. Barlow leaped and bowled all three Mexicans over, the four of them rolling in a heap of arms, legs and curses.

Hesitating only long enough to see that the last two Mexicans were backing away, faces frightened, White Bear waded into the pile. He grabbed a handful of hair and pulled up a little. Sure that it was a Mexican and not his friend, he smashed the side of the man's face with his war club.

He grabbed another handful of hair, and the annoyed grunt told him right away it was Barlow. "Sorry, old chap," he said as another Mexican popped his head up. He lashed out, and caught the man on the head, but high up, and the stone club skittered across the man's hair without doing much real damage.

Blanching, the man scrabbled backward on his rear end, wanting only to get away from these two raving lunatics. Out of reach of the deadly weapon, he shoved himself to his feet, turned and ran for the door. The two men who had not joined the fight hastily followed him.

Barlow and the third man from the pile rose at about the same time. The Mexican punched Barlow in the jaw, which did little more than make the former mountain man even angrier.

"That was a damn fool thing to do, hoss," Barlow growled, just before thumping his foe square in the center of the forehead with the pinky side of his right fist.

The Mexican reeled, and his eyes rolled up in his head. Then he fell to the floor, landing on his mangled friend.

Barlow pulled his knife and knelt, grabbing a bunch of the man's shirt and pulling him up a little. Just before he plunged the blade into the unfortunate foe, a voice rang out, "That'll be enough!"

Barlow looked up and saw an American Army sergeant and several privates heading toward him. The soldiers herded the three Mexicans who had run away in front of them. Barlow rose and slid the knife away.

Buffalo 2 left off chewing on the man he had attacked and, growling fiercely, edged up toward the soldiers.

"Buffler," Barlow said sharply. "C'mon over here, boy."

The dog stopped, released another snarl and then came over to stand at Barlow's side. He looked wary.

"What's this here ruckus all about, mister?" the sergeant asked, looking straight at Barlow.

"There's been a commotion here, hoss?" Barlow asked in mock innocence.

"Just answer the question, mister," the sergeant

snapped. "What happened here? What made you and your wild Injin friend over there turn this place into an abattoir?"

"Wild Indian?" White Bear asked. "Surely you don't mean me, old chap?"

The sergeant looked at him in surprise, shook his head, and then turned back to Barlow. "What's your name, mister?" he asked evenly.

"Will Barlow."

"I would be much obliged, Mister Barlow," the sergeant said in weary tones, "if you'd just tell me what went on here."

Barlow shrugged. "Them Mexican boys took exception to us for no reason I could fathom. That 'un over there," he said, pointing to the one Buffalo 2 had mauled, who was now on his feet, "smashed me in the back with a chair. Then the bastard tried to gut me. But ol' Buffler here, he come to the rescue." He looked down at the dog and patted his head. "Didn't you, boy?"

The man holding his arm, which seemed to be missing a considerable amount of meat, glowered at Barlow.

The sergeant stood in thought for a few moments, then nodded. "Seems reasonable to me that you and your redsk—Injin friend over there took exception to such treatment. We've had a lot of trouble from some of these greasers. Ain't a one of 'em can be trusted, as far as I've seen since I've been in this hellhole."

Barlow shrugged.

"Well, then, we'll just haul these damn boys off to jail and let the law deal with 'em."

"Ah, hell, Sergeant," Barlow said, "let 'em be. Two of 'em's gone under, and I reckon the others've learned a lesson with the thumpin' me and White Bear and Buffalo 2 gave 'em. I don't suppose they'll commence no more trouble."

The sergeant looked doubtful. "You sure that's what you want, Mister Barlow?"

"Reckon it is," Barlow said with a firm nod.

"All right, then." He turned to the Mexicans. "Get the hell outta here before I take you to jail just for the hell of it."

The men scrambled, running as fast as they were able.

"Grab them two dead ones, boys," the sergeant ordered.

His men moved to comply.

Barlow turned and, letting his anger slide away, grinned as he headed toward Rosaria. White Bear swiftly moved up to a warmly smiling Inez. The two men left the cantina, arm in arm with the two women. Snow was falling again, though lightly.

3

THE FOURSOME AND the dog stopped just outside the cantina. The wind blew steadily, though not strongly, bringing a deeper chill.

"Well, ladies, where away do we go?" Barlow asked.

"You have no rooms?" Rosaria asked, surprised.

"Nope. Ain't really had time to get any. We started lookin' for you two soon's we rode into town. Took us a spell before we found you."

"What about Viuda Garza's place, old chap?" White Bear asked, referring to the widow with whom they had taken rooms the last time they were in Taos.

"Reckon that'd do, hoss. If she'll have us."

"There is that, of course, mate. But she was a bloody good old lady, and I think she'll not object."

Barlow slid his rifle into a simple scabbard on his saddle. With Barlow towing Beelzebub, his sturdy mule, and White Bear his pony, the four strode off through the cold, light snow and wind. The only one who seemed to be enjoying the winter weather was Buffalo 2.

Within minutes, they were at a small, dangerously tilting adobe house. The men tied their animals up and Barlow knocked on the door.

A plump, white-haired old woman opened the door and her eyes widened in surprise. Then she smiled in delight. She rattled off several sentences in her own language.

"She welcomes you back to her home, *señores*," Rosaria translated.

Barlow nodded. "Ask her if she'll rent us a room again."

Viuda Garza nodded enthusiastically and stepped back to let her guests in. Inside, Barlow handed her several pesos. "That enough?" he asked.

Rosaria translated for Viuda Garza, whose firm nod needed no translating. The old woman showed them all to the small, cramped room at the rear of the house that they had used before. It looked the same as it had the first time they looked at it—two rickety beds, a nightstand, small bureau and on the wall a crucifix and a poor tin mirror. The only difference was that it appeared to have been cleaned recently, as if Viuda Garza had been expecting Barlow and White Bear to return.

"Are you hungry?" Viuda Garza asked in Spanish.

Rosaria translated and she and her three companions shook their heads.

With a smile, knowing the two men and two young women wanted to be alone, Viuda Garza smiled and backed out of the room, closing the door as she did.

Rosaria shrugged off her thick wool shawl and let it slip to the floor. There was no heat in the room, and she shivered slightly.

Barlow tugged off his capote and tossed it aside. "Here, now, *señorita*," he said with a grin, "let this ol' chil' warm you up some." He pulled her into his big, powerful arms and held her tenderly.

Warmth radiated from his body into hers, and Rosaria

rested her head on his broad chest. Under his shirt, she could feel the power of his muscles. And lower, through his pants, she could feel another kind of strength.

Barlow suddenly bent and scooped Rosaria easily up in his arms, turned and placed her gently on the rickety old bed. He eased himself onto the bed next to her, and kissed her softly, lengthily, hungrily.

She responded in kind, devouring his mouth and tongue, her body responding already.

Barlow's right hand moved down and began tugging at Rosaria's dress, pulling it up to where he could get his hand under it. His callused palm stroked her thighs, venturing near, but never quite touching her womanhood. Soon Rosaria was moaning quietly as Barlow gently nibbled at her neck and ears, teasing her, helping build up the fires that had started inside her.

Barlow then found her pleasure button and vigorously rubbed it in a circular motion. Rosaria gasped with the pleasure that had suddenly shot through her. Barlow continued his action, his finger moving from side to side, faster and faster.

Rosaria, who had had her arms around him, pulled his head close to her and kissed him hard. Within moments, her scream of ecstasy burst from her mouth and into his. Her body shook and tensed.

Before she had completely recovered from her climax, Barlow's hand was busy again, stroking, rubbing, entering, exiting. Rosaria's hips wriggled, and she ground her groin against his hand, like a cat insisting on being petted.

Climaxes came in little waves for her, crashing through her, and then receding. Up and down. Peaks and small valleys of excitement rolled over her, until she was gasping for breath.

"Stop," she finally whispered, pushing her face away from his a bit.

"I do somethin' wrong?" Barlow asked, surprised and a little disheartened.

"No, no, *mi corazón*. I just need to rest a moment and catch my breath."

"You sure that's all it is?" Barlow asked worriedly.

"*Sí.*" Rosaria grinned. "That and I want you in me *pronto*. ¡*Muy pronto!*"

"That, *señorita*, I can do for you!"

It still being rather chilly in the room, Barlow did not bother to undress, nor did he strip Rosaria. He simply undid his pants and pushed them down to his knees, and shoved Rosaria's dress up far enough so that he could slide up between her legs.

She smiled at him, her eyes burning with desire. "*Sí,*" she said. "Now is the time."

Barlow slid his manhood into her silky tunnel, moaning as thrills raced the length of him. He moved then, setting a strong, steady pace that Rosaria soon matched. Their speed quickened until their now-hot bodies were slamming together with mighty slaps.

"Good lord almighty!" Barlow suddenly shouted and he plunged almost fiercely into the woman.

Rosaria screamed out a steady stream of Spanish and she bucked and bounced with her own climax.

Breathing heavily, they lay on the bed, facing one another, smiling giddily, wordless now, basking in the warm glow of each other's passion. They paid no attention to White Bear and Inez, who were bouncing wildly on their own bed, threatening to make it collapse.

Soon, however, they, too, were quiet except for gasps as they tried to regain their breath.

"You all right over there, hoss?" Barlow called over his shoulder, grinning at Rosaria.

"More than all right, old chap. Damn fine, I'd say."

● ● ●

Barlow and White Bear stayed in Taos for a couple of weeks, enough to spend Christmas with their lovers and celebrate the holiday in Mexican style. Barlow did all right with it, until he spotted a little girl on the afternoon of Christmas Eve. The reminder of Anna sent him spinning into deep melancholy. He worried that winter would never end, that he would never find Anna, that his quest was hopeless. Even Rosaria's attentive, lustful, willing ministrations did little to shake his gloom.

When the Christmas festivities were over, however, Barlow's dark mood began to subside, and by the time the four welcomed in the new year, he had put aside the despondency for the most part.

New Year's Day, as Barlow and White Bear were sitting in a cantina downing coffee and trying to hold some food in their stomachs, suffering from massive hangovers, an Army officer approached.

"Mister Barlow?" Lieutenant Prescott Johnston asked.

"What'n hell do you want, hoss?" Barlow growled, glaring up with bleary eyes at the soldier.

"The captain would like you to take some dispatches down to Colonel Price in Santa Fe."

"I ain't of a mood, hoss. Now leave me the hell alone."

"I can't do that, sir. Captain Newberry expressly told me to find you and bring you to his office."

"You can tell Cap'n Newberry to go straight to hell, hoss," Barlow growled. It had been a long time since he had gotten this drunk, and he was not happy about having done it, and not only because of the hangover. He saw it as a weakness, and that irritated him.

"Mister Barlow," Johnston said with a sigh, "I'm afraid I must insist that you come with me."

"If you value your bloody life and hair, old chap," White Bear interjected, wincing as pain shot through his head, "you'll take yourself away from here and come see Will tomorrow."

"But I . . ."

"In about two seconds, this bloody large man sitting next to me is going to rise and smite your bloomin' arse down, old chap."

Lieutenant Johnston took a long look at Barlow, taking in the whiskey-bloated but still hard face, the large callused hands, the bull-like neck and massive torso. Plus there was the huge black dog at Barlow's feet, growling softly at the offense to his master. Johnston quickly decided that a strategic retreat to regroup and perhaps find reinforcements was the wisest course of action. He spun on his boot heel and marched stiffly out.

Barlow laid his head back onto his arms and moaned. White Bear followed his example, wondering why he had ever let Barlow talk him into drinking so much whiskey. This new year thing had nothing to do with him, and he knew what whiskey did to him. He sighed and dozed off.

Lieutenant Johnston found the two in the same cantina the next morning, but they were in much better shape—and humor. Still, Johnston had brought along a corporal and six soldiers, just in case. The officer cleared his throat, then said, "Captain Newberry would still like to see you, Mister Barlow. At your convenience," he added, though the implication in his voice meant that the commander wanted to see him immediately if not sooner.

Barlow finished off a shot of whiskey and pushed himself up. "Well, hoss," he said evenly, "now seems a right fine time for sich." He ignored the troops following behind him, White Bear and Buffalo 2 as they headed out to the adobe building across the plaza that Captain Newberry had commandeered for his headquarters.

"Glad you could make it, Barlow," Newberry said with

more than a touch of sarcasm, as Barlow and White Bear sat in chairs across from the officer. Newberry waved the lieutenant and his small detachment out of the room.

"We was occupied," Barlow said flatly, face showing nothing.

"So I understand," Newberry commented wryly. He paused, leaning back in his chair. Then he asked, "You seem to be fairly close to some of the people here, Barlow. Have you heard anything of trouble being planned by the Mexicans?"

Barlow shrugged. "Not really. One ol' hoss tol' me a few days ago that there was talk of the Mexicans and Taos Injins risin' up against the Americans hereabouts. But I ain't heard any more sich talk since then, and I ain't seen nothin' that would make me believe they're really plannin' sich a thing."

Newberry absorbed that, and then nodded. "I don't think these damned Mexicans have the spine to try something like that. And it's even more doubtful that the Injuns do," he said.

"If I hear anythin' else, Cap'n, I'll let you know," Barlow said, starting to rise.

"That'll be difficult, Barlow, since you'll be in Santa Fe, at least for a spell."

"What's that?" Barlow asked plunking himself back into the chair.

"I need you to take some dispatches and reports to Colonel Price in Santa Fe." He paused, then added, "They're very important."

"They always are," Barlow said sarcastically, forcing White Bear to stifle a snorty laugh.

Newberry glowered. "You'll leave as soon as you get your horse . . ."

"Mule," Barlow corrected.

". . . mule saddled. Stop back here and I'll have everything ready."

"I don't think so, hoss," Barlow said flatly. "Me'n
White Bear here got us some business to finish up here
in Taos."

"Such as?"

"That ain't none of your concern," Barlow said, thinking of at least one more night with the delectable Rosaria.

"It is when it affects Army business, Barlow," Newberry snapped. He hated dealing with civilians. They were
usually insolent, and Will Barlow was one of the worse.

"Don't get your balls in a knot, hoss," Barlow said.
"We'll leave out first light tomorrow. There ain't nothin'
in them papers you got that cain't wait a day before bein'
sent out."

Captain Newberry also hated being put off. As far as
he was concerned, his business—Army business—always
came first. But he knew he could not force Barlow to
change his mind. The man was too obstinate, and would
probably go to jail before being made to do something he
wasn't ready for. Newberry nodded. "All right, then, Barlow. Just make sure you're here at dawn."

"Or thereabouts," Barlow said, biting back a smile. He
rose. "Anythin' else, hoss?"

"You're dismissed."

As Barlow, White Bear and Buffalo 2 left, the Shoshoni
said, "You do get quite a bit of merriment out of baiting
such people, don't you, old chap?"

Barlow looked at his friend and just grinned widely.

The two men and the dog went straight back to Viuda
Garza's house, where Barlow told the Mexican woman
that they would be pulling out the next morning. The
white-haired widow nodded, somewhat sad. She liked
these two men, and would miss them.

"I reckon we'll be back again afore long," Barlow said,

making the old woman smile once more. Then he and White Bear headed to the room they shared, where Rosaria and Inez waited. The women were not happy to hear that the men were leaving, but they were assuaged by promises of return, tender words and powerfully lusty ministrations.

4

AS THEY WERE leaving Captain Newberry's office the next morning, Barlow and White Bear saw Manuel Ortega.

"Leavin'?" the Mexican asked.

Barlow nodded. "More papers for the Army. Goddamn soldiers generate more useless pieces of paper than any people I ever saw."

"Will you come back?"

"Reckon so," Barlow agreed. "There are certain amenities here that this ol' hoss enjoys partakin' of."

"Of course the same could be said of Santa Fe, old chap," White Bear offered with a grin on his dark face.

"That's a fact, hoss. It purely is." Barlow looked at Ortega. "You heard anythin' else about that matter you mentioned when we rode into town here?"

Ortega shook his head. "Just more grumblings of discontent."

Barlow nodded. "Well, you watch your ass, hoss. If them boys start somethin', you stay out of it, hear? Even if the Mexicans and Taoseños do work together, they ain't gonna win. They might be able to take Taos back—for a spell. But word'll git out fast as a cat strikin' and the whole goddamn American Army will be here in days. And I reckon they won't be none too pleased with sich doin's."

"I think you are right, *amigo*," Ortega said with a nod. "I hadn't figured to join them, for much the same reasons."

"Good. And, if there is fightin', hoss, you cache and lay low. If the Army ends up ridin' here to put down a revolt, any Mexican male is gonna be in danger. I'd hate for you to git shot jist 'cause you're a Mexican."

Ortega nodded again. He didn't like the thought that he might be a target just because of his heritage, but he could understand it. If a revolt broke out in Taos, Americans would be fair game, even if they were not among the real oppressors of the Mexican people. *"Vaya con dios,"* he said.

"Gracias." Barlow pulled himself into Beelzebub's saddle while White Bear hopped onto his pony. *"Adios,"* Barlow said as he and the Shoshoni walked the animals out of the plaza, heading toward the road to Santa Fe. As usual, Buffalo 2 was wandering around out in front of the two riders, sniffing the ground and the air, glad to be out of the confines of the city, enjoying the cool air and the steady breeze that ruffled his fur.

They rode warily, remembering the attack on them on the trip north. But this time the journey was uneventful. They skirted the pueblos, just as a precaution, and made fair time considering they ran into a snow squall or two. They arrived in Santa Fe five days after leaving Taos, riding straight to the office that Colonel Sterling Price used as his headquarters while construction on Fort Marcy progressed.

White Bear and Buffalo 2 waited outside while Barlow

entered the building and handed the sack of reports, records and other items to the officer.

"I'd be obliged if you'd be within my reach for the next day or so, Mister Barlow," Price said. "I doubt there's anything in here," he added, tapping the leather pouch, "that'll need an immediate reply, but just in case there is, I'll need to get ahold of you in a hurry."

"We'll be at the same place as before," he said. "You remember where that is?"

Price nodded.

Barlow walked out, and then he and his two companions—one human, one canine—headed toward the cantina where their lady friends worked for Lupe's fat old grandfather. They were eager to see the women. Rosaria was plumb shinin', as far as Barlow was concerned, but there was something extra special about Natividad. He suspected White Bear felt the same about Lupe, though they had never really discussed it.

Natividad and Lupe seemed as overjoyed to see them as the men were to see the women. They rushed forward and jumped into the men's arms, wrapping their arms around the men's necks, and their legs around their middles. Each man was greeted with a large, sloppy wet kiss before the women slid back to their feet on the floor.

"I was hopin' you would've missed me some whilst I was gone," Barlow said with a big grin.

"Oh, you," Natividad said, slapping him playfully on the arm.

Barlow's grin widened even more. "Can you leave here?"

"*Sí,*" Natividad said eagerly. She and Lupe went to get their thick, heavy serapes and then rejoined the men. Outside, the men mounted their animals, and pulled the women up behind them. Then they rode toward the plain, somewhat run-down adobe house they had all shared during the time Barlow and White Bear had been in Santa Fe.

They wasted no time in getting unclothed and beginning to enjoy each other's fleshly delights. Moans and groans of pleasure soon banged around the walls, escaping through some small cracks in the adobe to flee outside and be swept away by the winter wind.

A loud thumping on the door the next morning roused Barlow from a sound and peaceful sleep. Grumbling, he rose, slid into his fringed buckskin pants and headed for the door. He was scowling as he opened it.

The glower deepened when he saw Sergeant Preston Smalls standing there with half a dozen soldiers.

"Colonel Price requests you attend on him now, sir," Smalls said officiously.

"Piss on him," Barlow snapped, starting to close the door.

Smalls kicked it back open and ordered his men into firing position. "He said *now*, Mister Barlow, and I aim to make sure that's when you go there."

Stony faced, Barlow glared at the soldiers. "You know, hoss," he said tightly, "if the colonel's all that fired up to see me about somethin', I don't think it'd shine with him for you boys to shoot me down dead."

Smalls hadn't really thought of that. He had never met a man who stood there so coolly and calmly with six guns pointed at him. He had expected Barlow to just give in when his life appeared to be in danger. It was what any other man would do.

"I suppose you're right about that," Smalls said, anger building in him. "Put up your weapons, boys." He glared at Barlow. "But he didn't say we couldn't damage you some, then tie you up and drag your sorry ass over there."

Smalls was shocked again at Barlow's reaction. He had

expected a contrite apology and an agreement to come along quietly. Instead, Barlow reared back his head and let out a laugh that built up in his ample belly, charged up through the huge chest and out.

"I say something funny, mister?" Smalls asked, enraged.

"Git your ass out of here, hoss," Barlow said, chuckles still bubbling inside. "Go on back to Colonel Price and tell him I'll be along when I git the urge, which shouldn't be more'n a couple hours."

"I can't do that, sir," Smalls said. He was determined now to teach this massive block of a man a lesson in taking orders. He was so furious that he did not take note of the scars that marred Barlow's huge chest, each one gotten from an enemy, not by accident.

"Then you're gonna git hurt, hoss," Barlow said, all joviality slipping away from him.

Smalls stepped aside, just outside the door. "Take him, men," he ordered.

The soldiers charged, but they could only get through one at a time. The first one to try to enter was greeted by a crushing blow to the face from Barlow's big right hand. So much power did it contain, that it knocked the soldier back into his fellows, and all six went backward and fell. The first lay on the ground, soft moans bubbling from his bloody, mangled lips.

Barlow stepped out. Warily watching the soldiers, he half turned and grabbed Sergeant Smalls by the front of his tunic. "That was a goddamn fool thing to do, hoss," Barlow growled. He slammed the blue-coated soldier against the wall, eliciting a sharp grunt of pain.

He was about to repeat the maneuver when two soldiers jumped on his back, one with an arm around the massive neck, the other with both arms around Barlow's right arm.

Both tugged and squeezed, trying to pull him away from their sergeant.

But all they accomplished was making the big man even angrier. Barlow dropped Smalls, turned and took two quick steps backward, smashing the two soldiers' backs against the house, with all the weight of his blocky body behind it. The soldiers released their grip on him and sank to the ground in pain.

Barlow spun and brought his right arm up fast, smashing a charging trooper in the face with the forearm. The soldier stopped in his tracks, then dropped straight down in an untidy pile.

Barlow swiftly surveyed the battlefield. White Bear had just clubbed one of the soldiers to the ground, and Buffalo 2 was holding the last soldier at bay. With a nod, Barlow turned back to Smalls. He grabbed the sergeant by the throat and squeezed.

White Bear hurried over and punched Barlow none too lightly on the left biceps. "Let him be, old chap," he said urgently.

"Why?"

"Because Colonel Price will lock your bloody sorry arse up in the gaol, mate, where you'll languish until you are bloomin' hanged, that's why," White Bear explained. "You know these army people. They're not amused by having their sergeants killed by raving mountain men."

"Reckon you're right, hoss." He glared at Smalls's very worried face. "Of course, the army might not mind was I to jist thump him a little and then tie him up and drag his ass over back there."

"I suppose they won't mind as much with that. Probably not more than a few bloody weeks in the gaol."

"Harumph," Barlow snorted. He released Smalls's throat, and the man fell back a little, resting against the wall of the house while trying to regain his breath. "Next time you go agin somebody, boy, don't be so goddamn cocky 'cause you outnumber 'em. Next time you jist might git kilt. You ever come agin me again, and that'll be a fact." He took a step backward. "Now you and your boys jist sit here till I'm ready to go, hoss. Me'n White Bear'll escort you back to Colonel Price's."

"We can make it," Smalls gargled.

"I misdoubt that, hoss." He entered the house, the anger gone already. He grinned and winked at Natividad. Then he dressed and headed back out. White Bear had donned his clothes before slipping out the back and coming up from behind the soldiers to join the fight, so he was ready.

The two men helped the conscious soldiers onto their horses and then tossed the three unconscious ones over their saddles. Barlow and White Bear mounted their animals, unsaddled, and herded the soldiers before them as they rode toward the plaza. Soldiers and civilians watched in surprise—and some with considerable glee—as the small, uncommon parade marched past.

Another sergeant was standing in front of Price's headquarters, watching the procession with interest. When they stopped, he shook his head. "Trouble?" he asked.

"They fell off their horses," Barlow said flatly.

"All of 'em?" the sergeant asked incredulously. Then he nodded in understanding. "You're here to see Colonel Price?"

Barlow nodded and slid off the mule, and White Bear off his pony.

"I'll tell him you're here." He turned and went inside, then returned in less than a minute. "He's expecting you, Mister Barlow."

"Obliged," Barlow said politely. With White Bear and Buffalo 2 at his side, he went inside as the sergeant began ordering men to help the injured soldiers.

When the two visitors had sat, Price asked, "I understand my men fell off their horses?" There was no belief in his voice.

"Yep. Damn poor riders you got there, Colonel, was you to ask me," Barlow said evenly.

"Well, at least you didn't kill any of them," Price said wearily.

"Why'd you want to see me, Colonel? It don't shine with me to be disturbed from my slumbers fer no good reason. I hope you got one."

Price picked up a sheet of paper from his desk. "This was among the dispatches you brought from Taos," he said quietly. "And I don't like its implications."

"What's it say?"

"That talk of revolution is rife in Taos. That the Mexicans and some of the Injuns nearby are stockpiling weapons for an assault on the town, and then a march down here. There's talk, too, Captain Newberry says, that the remnants of the Mexican army might be on their way to help the insurrectionists."

"Cap'n Newberry is a worrywart," Barlow said with a snort.

"What do you know of this?"

"Not much. Jist what I told him. A Mexican friend told me'n White Bear that there was some talk of a revolt. Jist as we was leavin' Taos, we talked with him. He's heard no more talk. And certainly nothin' about the goddamn Mexican army showin' up. I imagine them boys're so deep into Mexico now that'd take 'em months to git back here even if they was of a mind to."

"Do you trust this Mexican friend of yours, Mister Barlow?"

"I do, Colonel." He paused, then added, "I ain't sure why Cap'n Newberry wrote that. Jist before we left, when we talked with him, he said he was sure neither the Mexicans nor the Taoseños had the spine to rise up agin us Americans."

"What do you think about that?" Price asked.

Barlow shrugged. "Cain't never tell with people, Colonel. I know the Mexicans resent you bein' here, and they ain't fond of losin' a good portion of their country. I suppose anybody'd rise up agin an oppressor, given enough reason to. Whether this is reason enough, hell, I don't know."

Price sat in thought for a bit. Finally he made up his mind. "I suppose I can wait a spell on this, then." He still seemed a little worried, though.

"Reckon that'd be best," Barlow said. "At least till you was to get more information—more definite information—that the Mexicans are commencin' trouble."

Price nodded. "I might need you to take more dispatches up to Taos in the next day or so, Mister Barlow."

"Hell, Colonel, I jist got back here and got things to see to," Barlow complained.

"Like some women, I suppose," Price commented with a knowing grin.

Barlow smiled.

"All right, I'll find someone else. But, if you decide to go anywhere, let me know. I will need you to make another trip up there eventually."

Barlow nodded, rose, and with White Bear and Buffalo 2, left.

5

BARLOW AND WHITE Bear settled in with Natividad and Lupe in the rickety adobe house a few blocks from the Santa Fe plaza. Here, each man had his own room, unlike Viuda Garza's place in Taos. There was also a decent-size kitchen. Both Natividad and Lupe were great cooks, and so they all ate well, as Barlow kept the pantry filled. He had managed to finally get some money out of the Army for his services, and while he watched his spending, he did not mind putting out pesos to keep himself and his friends in vittles.

The men never asked how the women were able to stay away from home or get out of helping in the cantina for days at a time. The men didn't care. They just cared that Natividad and Lupe were there and lusty.

The rooms were, as far as Barlow and White Bear considered it, quite comfortable, at least compared to many of the other places they had spent the night. Despite the dilapidated exterior of the house, the inside was relatively posh by Santa Fe standards. Each room had its own wooden bed covered with a goosedown tick and several warm blankets. There was a nightstand, a bureau with a washbasin and a ewer. A chamber pot rested under each bed, so they would not have to go outside during the bitter nights. There was also a small *horno*—the ubiquitous adobe fireplaces that also served as ovens.

Winter seemed to get harsher, with the wind often gusting heavily, threatening to knock the old house down, and snow fell fitfully. But the two men didn't much care about that either. It was warm enough in the adobe house, what with the small stoves in the rooms. Even better, it was hot in the beds; Natividad and Lupe made sure of that.

Life was comfortable here and Barlow found himself getting rather lazy and complacent. So when another knock on the door woke him one morning, he grumbled only a little as he pulled on his pants and went to answer it. He was a little taken aback when he opened the door and saw a nervous, frightened soldier, who was sweating despite the cold temperatures. He was holding the reins to a lathered horse.

"What can I do for you, hoss?" Barlow asked.

"Colonel Price wants to see you right away, sir," the private said breathlessly, almost as if he had been running. "He said to tell you it's very important."

"You have any idear what's goin' on, boy?" Barlow asked, his puzzlement—and concern—growing.

"There's been a revolt up in Taos, sir," the soldier said, his breath slowing some. "The Mexicans and some Injins from one of the pueblos up that way went on the rampage. From word we got, they even killed and scalped Governor Bent right in his own home. In front of his wife and young'uns."

"Good Lord Almighty," Barlow whispered. He paused, thinking, then asked, "You have any more errands to run?"

"Yessir. I've more people I have to notify."

"Then go about it, hoss. I'll get myself on over to the colonel's directly."

The private jumped onto his horse and galloped off. Barlow turned back into the house. White Bear and the two women were standing there, the Shoshoni wearing only his pants, the two women wrapped in blankets. "You heard, hoss?" Barlow asked.

White Bear nodded. He turned and headed toward his room. Barlow stalked past the suddenly frightened women toward his own room. There he swiftly dressed and gathered up his weapons. By the time he stepped back into the kitchen and headed for the door, White Bear was right behind him, followed by Buffalo 2. Again the two men mounted their riding animals bareback and trotted toward the plaza, and Colonel Price's headquarters.

The plaza was buzzing with activity, chaos apparently reigning. Men ran around seemingly without purpose, while others gathered in groups around horses or mules, some loading supplies, others just waiting, puffing on pipes or shuck cigarillos.

Barlow and White Bear left their animals out of the way of the worst of the pandemonium and bulled their way through the crowds toward the Army headquarters. Finally they managed to make their way into Price's office, where it was peaceful and quiet.

"You got the news, I presume?" the colonel asked without preliminary. When Barlow nodded, Price said, "I'm putting together a small force to send up north, Mister Barlow. I can't afford to send too many men. I might need most of them here. Since this one 'rumor' has proven true, others—like the Mexican army marching back here—might also be true."

Barlow nodded. There was no need to say anything.

"I figure you'd want to go and help set things right up there, Mister Barlow."

Barlow nodded again. He didn't have many friends in Taos, but he knew some of the men there from the mountain days. Besides, just the thought of what had been done to Charles Bent, a man he didn't know but had heard much of, angered him.

"Go see a man named Ceran St. Vrain. He has a store in town, as well as one up in Taos, and he's putting together a party of men like you, Mister Barlow. Former mountain men and such. You might consider going with him."

Barlow nodded again. "You won't need me?"

"No, Mister Barlow."

"How do I find this St. Vrain feller?"

"Look for a bossy little Frenchman," Price said, almost smiling. "Short man, big black beard."

"Doesn't sound like much of a leader to me, Colonel," Barlow allowed.

"He's been out here a good many years. Started up in the mountain trade just like you did, taking and trading beaver. He may be lacking in height, but he's as big and as tough as any man west of the Mississippi River."

Barlow nodded and turned to leave, but stopped and spun back when Price called him.

"One more thing, Mister Barlow. St. Vrain is—was— Governor Bent's partner. Had been for quite some years. They were, in addition, close friends. That's why he is leading the foray to Taos."

Barlow's eyes widened in surprise, then he nodded. He and White Bear went outside and began looking for a dark-haired, dark-bearded man. As they stomped along, Barlow suddenly heard some excited, angry streams of French. He turned toward the sound and after some men had moved, spotted the man he assumed to be Ceran St. Vrain. He walked over and tapped the still shouting Frenchman on the shoulder.

St. Vrain turned to look at him, and stopped jabbering. "What you want, *monsieur*?" he asked. "*Je suis trés busy.*"

"I aim to go with you to Taos, hoss," Barlow said flatly. "Me and my friend White Bear and good ol' Buffler."

"Is he a Shoshoni?" St. Vrain asked.

"Yes, I am, old chap," White Bear answered for himself.

St. Vrain's eyes widened. Then he almost grinned through his grief and anger. "*Bien,*" he said with a slight bow. He turned to Barlow. "You're an old mountaineer, yes, *monsieur*?" he asked.

"Yep."

"*Bienvenue, monsieurs.* We leave in three-quarters of an hour, *mes amis.* Be here zen. If you need somet'ing, like ball or powder, zis is my store 'ere. You can get what you need from my clerks. Ze clerks will also give you some jerked meat and hardtack, *ça va*?"

Barlow and White Bear nodded. They hurried back to their animals and trotted back to their house. There they said good-bye to Natividad and Lupe in a most manly fashion, even though they were quite rushed. Dressed again, they grabbed their sleeping robes and an extra pair of moccasins each, and their possible bags, and headed outside. There each saddled his own riding animal, tied their small possible sacks on, and rode back to the plaza.

They needed only a few minutes in St. Vrain's store—which was just about empty now, since most of the other men had already gotten what they needed—and stocked up on the few supplies they thought they might need. Then they went outside and waited amid the still-swirling, dusty tumult.

St. Vrain led his group out of the plaza soon afterward. The motley bunch of fifty or so rawhide-tough men presented a hell of a procession as they went: Frenchmen and

Americans who, like St. Vrain had been in Mexico for years; other former mountain men, American, French-Canadian, Irish, Scots, dressed much like they had in the old days, in buckskin and fur and heavy blanket coats; others, like White Bear, dressed Taos style, with wool pants and short, tight-fitting jackets and thick, wool serapes; still others were clad in whatever pants and coats they had been wearing when they got the word. Most of the men wore wide-brimmed felt hats with round crowns, though some wore hats of wolf, coyote or bobcat fur; a few wore small sombreros; a few just pulled up the hoods on their capotes.

All the men were heavily armed. Each carried a heavy short-barreled rifle, most from their mountain days, trusted weapons that they knew well. Quite a few had double-barreled shotguns in scabbards, for an emergency. And each sported an assortment of pistols—single-shot muzzleloaders; similar but bigger, heaver horse pistols; some, like Barlow, carried five-shot Colt Paterson revolving pistols. Plus each toted an assortment of knifes and tomahawks. About the only one who stood out because of his arms was White Bear, who carried his bow and quiver of arrows across his back. He had, however, made some concessions and had a shotgun tied to his simple saddle, and a single-shot pistol jammed into his belt, within easy reach under the serape.

They were, to a man, grim of face, and determined of intent. They were out for blood, to avenge the men they had known, trapped with, traded with, drank with, gambled and yarned with. Men who had died at the hands of a bloodthirsty mob of—to them—foreigners.

For a bunch of hardy, independent men, they were surprisingly constrained on the ride, accepting orders willingly if not with great appreciation. Of course, it helped that St. Vrain and his two lieutenants gave few orders.

All of these men were used to traveling in harsh conditions and on tough missions. They knew the trail routine so well they could do most of it in their sleep, which there was precious little of on this journey. They didn't race along, but St. Vrain had set a steady, ground-covering pace that would have them in Taos in a little over three days, unless something went wrong.

The Army column followed St. Vrain's group, but the independent force worried not a bit about the soldiers. The blue coats could make their own way and time on the trail. St. Vrain and his men were eager to get to Taos and begin avenging the loss of their friends.

St. Vrain's men rode until well after dark that first night, tended the animals, wolfed down some jerky, hardtack and water, and then turned in, exhausted.

They were on the move again, after another cold, tasteless meal, before dawn had really broken. Despite their tiredness and lack of decent food, the men's determination never flagged. It would take far more than a few long days in the saddle and several poor meals to have them begin to doubt the righteousness of their mission.

Buffalo 2 trotted along with the group, seemingly unconcerned about the long hours on the move. He generally plodded along off to one side—the side nearest where Barlow and White Bear rode, glancing over at the two men now and again to make sure they were still there.

They made another cold camp well after dark, and once again were on the move before dawn had broken. Still no one grumbled. The soldiers were nowhere in sight.

Along about noon, the few Indians other than White Bear who were along—mostly Delawares—rode back to the column. They had been out scouting, as they had been since leaving Santa Fe.

St. Vrain stopped the group and stood in his stirrups to address the men. "Ze scouts tell me zere are some of ze rebels not too far ahead of us. We will attack zem as soon as we can, and show zem that ze way zey have chosen is ze wrong way."

Shots, catcalls and even a few war whoops erupted from the men. Barlow and White Bear did not join in the cacophony, seeing no real reason to do so. They would fight as hard as anyone when the time came.

The group moved on, slower, wary yet eager to join the battle. They were quiet now. The soldiers were still nowhere to be seen behind them, but the men did not care. They wanted this fight to be theirs, without interference from the Army.

St. Vrain stopped them when they edged up onto a snow-covered wide spot along the trail that was too rocky to be called a meadow. "I think zis is where zey will attack," St. Vrain said to those nearest him, and word quickly filtered back to everyone.

"Waugh!" one of the old mountain men shouted. "Let's jus' ride on out there and make wolf bait out of them sons a bitches!"

That idea was loudly seconded by a considerable number of the men.

St. Vrain turned his horse to face the men. "Zat is foolish," he shouted. "But we will flush zem out." He spoke with a few of his men near him, and they chose several other men and rode off into the trees on the one side of the well-defined road and disappeared.

A quarter of an hour later, there were shouts from the other side of the meadow. Then a group of men burst out of the trees and rocks there, a few of them on horseback, most of them on foot.

"Now, *monsieurs*!" St. Vrain shouted. *"Vite! Vite!"* He kicked his horse and it took off. The others followed, racing along behind him, soon overtaking the squat, fierce-eyed Frenchman.

"Stay here, Buffler," Barlow shouted as he smacked his heels into Beelzebub's sides, goading the mule into a run. He hoped the dog would listen. He did not want the animal getting hurt. He glanced over and saw that White Bear was pacing him, his bow now out and strung, an arrow nocked, and three more arrows in his left hand, held against the bow.

6

AS INDEPENDENT MINDED as this group of fighting men was, they did not form a cohesive unit. But all had been in many a battle, and many had fought alongside others who were there now. All knew what to do, even if they were not planning to do it with military precision.

One surprise was the size of the force they were facing. Men seemed to continuously boil out of the trees and rocks, until there were a little more than a hundred on the field. But they were poorly armed, though they still carried the rage of revolution inside them. They clearly hated the Americans and wanted them all dead, if possible, or fleeing the rebels' retaken country.

The Americans didn't give a damn how many of the revolutionaries they faced. They were cocky, certain of their abilities, devoid of fear—and their determination was unshakable.

Barlow and White Bear slapped their animals into a run, racing side by side toward some of the few mounted rebels. To their flank, the Americans let loose a volley of gunfire, dropping a number of charging foes.

Barlow split away from White Bear and headed for a small knot of five rebellious men who were riding hard toward the one flank of his American companions. Leaving his rifle where it was in the loop at the front of his saddle, he pulled his two horse pistols, guiding the running mule only by knee pressure. When he was within about twenty yards of the group, Barlow fired one pistol, then the other.

One of the Mexicans coming at him sagged to the side on his horse, holding on for all he was worth. He tried to stop the horse and stay on top of it while his life drained away through the hole in his chest and the larger one in his back. He soon lost that fight and slipped off the horse. His foot caught in the stirrup and he was dragged, already dead, for a few yards before his boot popped off and he tumbled to a stop. His horse kept running, following the others.

"Dammit," Barlow swore, long before the dead man ended up on the ground. He was angry at himself for missing his second shot. He jammed the pistols back into the saddle holsters and pulled his belt pistols, firing right away, without aiming much.

He was a little surprised when he saw two bloody spots appear on one man's serape. The Mexican slumped forward, dead, lying alongside the horse's neck, flopping like a pile of rags in a windstorm.

The three remaining Mexicans split to go around Barlow, since they were sure this *loco americano* was going to crash right into them if they didn't. One slid by close enough that Barlow was able to clout him on the temple with a pistol barrel. The man sagged, but stayed on his mount.

Barlow stuffed his pistols into his belt as best he could, grabbed the reins and pulled Beelzebub to a sharp halt.

"C'mon, mule," he roared as he turned the animal. "We got to catch those boys."

The mule responded, leaping forward. The animal might not have been as fleet as the horses the Mexicans were riding, but he was powerful and had a lot more heart and stamina.

Then Barlow saw one of his companions frantically waving at him to get out of the line of fire. He jerked the mule to the left and kept running. A volley of gunfire exploded behind him. He looked over his shoulder and saw the three remaining Mexicans go down. He nodded grimly.

He pulled Beelzebub to a halt, and let the animal breathe a moment as he surveyed the field. Rebels were still flooding the field, but they were being cut down regularly. A mass of them on foot had reached the Americans, many of whom had slid off their horses and were beginning to battle the Mexicans—and some Indians, Barlow noticed—hand to hand. Though outnumbered, the Americans looked like they were holding on quite well for the time being.

He could not see White Bear, though he was not concerned about that. But fifty yards away, Barlow saw a fast-riding Mexican heading for another former trapper who had ridden off from the group. He was already fighting off two other rebels. A third would likely be too much.

Barlow slapped the mule's rump and raced toward the man, whose name he did not even know. It was enough that he was one of St. Vrain's party. Barlow pulled out his rifle, tried to aim, and fired. "Good goddamn," he muttered. As was often the case firing from the back of a swift-running animal, he missed.

As he galloped closely past the companion, he managed to whack one of the Mexicans he was fighting on the head with his rifle. It wasn't a hard blow, but it was enough to knock the man to the ground, giving the American another instant to take care of his second foe.

The mounted man coming at him was an Indian, Barlow noticed, and had a bone-head war club in his hand. As their animals' noses passed each other in opposite directions, the warrior swung the war club, and Barlow swung his rifle from a fully extended arm.

The club, which had teeth chipped into the bone, caught Barlow a glancing blow on the inside of the arm just above the elbow. But his rifle smashed the Indian backward. With his feet still in the stirrups, the warrior lay flat on his back across the horse's rump, bouncing like a bag of grain on a raft shooting the rapids. He could not pull himself up or get the horse to stop, since the reins were dragging along the ground.

Barlow pulled to a stop again, not caring about the Indian. The warrior was out of the battle for now, and could not hurt any of his friends. He began reloading his guns, keeping half an eye on the battlefield. The fight seemed to be winding down. Rebels were fleeing back toward the trees and rocks whence they came. Some were cut down by more gunfire from the American line; a few others were killed by the few men who had flushed them out in the first place.

Suddenly Beelzebub's knees buckled and the mule dropped like a stone. On his way down, Barlow heard the crack of a rifle. He managed to get his feet out of his stirrups, almost as if by instinct. He hit the ground and rolled. Grabbing his rifle, he crawled to the mule, which was still alive but suffering mightily. Barlow peeked over the mule's heaving side and spotted a rebel hastily trying to reload.

Anger surging through him, Barlow rose to one knee and carefully aimed his rifle. There was an explosion and a big puff of smoke. When that cleared, the rebel was on the ground and not moving. "Son of a bitch," Barlow muttered. "Kill my ol' mule on me, will you?"

He stood, and only then did he notice that his leg was bleeding, just below the bottom of his buttocks-length blanket coat. He ignored it for the time being. Sadly, Barlow pulled out a pistol, placed it against Beelzebub's head, and pulled the trigger, putting the animal out of its misery. It was not quite the same as it was when the first Buffalo was killed, but he would miss the steady, sturdy mule.

He reloaded his weapons in the quiet that had come with the end of the battle. Then he undid and tugged free his saddle, which was a lot of work, even for as strong a man as he was, what with that big old mule half laying on it.

Barlow sat on the saddle and stretched out his right leg. Swiftly he slit his buckskin pants a little and opened them.

"Is it bad, old chap?" White Bear asked, riding up.

"Jist a scratch. Winged me, and then kilt ol' Beelzebub."

"Better that bloody mule than you, mate," White Bear said firmly.

"Reckon so." Barlow looked up. "Go catch me up one of them damn rebels' horses, so's I got me somethin' to ride, hoss," he ordered quietly.

White Bear nodded and rode off. Barlow pulled a cloth shirt out of his possibles bag and cut a strip off the bottom. He wrapped it around the oozing, but not very deep, wound and tied it tightly. Then he sat and waited for White Bear, ignoring the pain in his leg, but unable to put aside the anger he felt at having lost his trusty mule.

The Shoshoni returned in minutes with a horse in tow. "I brought you a sturdy one, old chap," he said with a grin. "What with your bloody mass and all."

"I'm overwhelmed by your thoughtfulness," Barlow

said sarcastically. Though the horse was saddled, Barlow pulled that off and put his own saddle on the animal.

The two rode back to where the rest of the American force had gathered. Barlow kept going, riding around the side of the group, and back down the trail a little. There Buffalo 2 waited for him, seemingly anxious. When he saw his master, the dog's tail went wild, wagging with such force that it shook the whole back half of his body.

Barlow dismounted and knelt, petting the big New-foundland on the head. "Good boy," he said quietly but enthusiastically. "Yes, good boy, Buffler. I'm glad you did what I tol' you. I'd never forgive myself if I had lost you, too, boy. All right, c'mon, Buffler," Barlow said as he mounted the horse. "Let's go."

But the dog eased up toward the horse. He knew this was not Beelzebub, and wanted his nose to identify the animal. The horse, for its part, did not like the dog sniffing around him like that and shuffled considerably.

"That's enough, Buffler," Barlow said. "It ain't Beelzebub, but it'll have to do, so git used to this critter. Now, let's go."

The Americans had one man killed and several wounded, though none badly. The men crowed among themselves, whooping and hollering at their victory.

After a few minutes of that, St. Vrain mounted his horse and shouted, "Zat is enough, men. Zis is not ze time for frolicking and making merry. We still 'ave a long ride ahead of us, *ne-c'est pas*? Or 'ave you forgotten why we are going to Taos? Eh? Is zat it? If so, I will give you a reminder of why. Just remember *mon grand ami*, Charles Bent."

Without another word, he turned his horse and began moving out. Silently, the men mounted their own horses and followed along, quite subdued now, their glee at the victory swiftly forgotten.

● ● ●

They rode into Taos late the next morning to find that the
fighting was over and the rebellion put down for all in-
tents and purposes. When the Army column arrived the
next day and learned those facts, they moved on north
toward the Taos Pueblo, where many of the rebels were
holed up. For much of that day, the Army's two small
cannon blasted the pueblos. Eventually the leaders of the
revolt surrendered and were marched back to town.

St. Vrain and several other officious-looking men approached Barlow in a cantina the day after the rebel leaders were brought back into the city. The four men sat, at
Barlow's invitation. He was curious as to what St. Vrain
and the others wanted.

" 'Ow is your leg, *Monsieur* Barlow?" St. Vrain asked.

"Ain't but a scratch, Mister St. Vrain."

"Ah, *très bien, mon ami*." He paused, then went on. "I
want to t'ank you for your efforts with our force on ze
way up 'ere from Santa Fe."

"I was jist but one ol' hoss among many." Barlow
paused, looking hard at St. Vrain. "Jist what did you really
come here for, Mister St. Vrain?"

The Frenchman gave off the barest hint of a smile.
"Well, *mon ami*, I did want to t'ank you. Like all ze others, *ça va*? But zere is another reason, yes, that I look for
you. I . . ."

"Jist a minute, hoss," Barlow said. He called for a new
bottle of whiskey and some glasses. When they were
brought, he poured each man a glassful of the harsh li-
quor. "To our success, boys," Barlow said, raising his
glass in a toast.

The others followed suit, and they all drank a bit. Barlow set his glass down. "Now, Mister St. Vrain, what is
it you want from this ol' chil'?"

"We want to do zis the proper way," St. Vrain started.

"By American laws. So we are putting together a jury for ze trial of ze leaders of zis revolt. *Zut!* Damn!"

"That seems reasonable," Barlow said tentatively. "But what's that got to do with me?"

"We would like you to sit on zis jury, *monsieur*," St. Vrain said bluntly.

"Why me?"

"You 'ave no real connections 'ere, so you will be considered impartial."

"You don't believe that booshwa, do you, hoss?" Barlow asked, surprised at the statement.

"Non," St. Vrain said flatly.

"So it would give the appearance of bein' an impartial man on the jury?"

"Oui."

Barlow shrugged. "I'll ask you again, hoss—why me? There's a heap of other boys come up here with you, Mister St. Vrain."

The Frenchman grinned grimly. "You were one of ze few men wounded during zat engagement on ze trail, *monsieur*. Zat and ze fact zat you are still somet'ing of an outsider to ze parts make you perfect for zis task."

Barlow thought about it, though it didn't take long. He had no real reason to refuse. He had no love for the men who had revolted against American rule. They had killed a number of good people and deserved everything they got. "All right, Mister St. Vrain," he said slowly. "I cain't see no reason not to help you out here."

"Très bien! Très bien!" St. Vrain said jubilantly. "After seeing you in ze battle ze other day, I knew I could count on you, *monsieur*. Ze trial, it starts ze day after tomorrow, in ze old *alcalde's* office."

"I'll be there," Barlow promised.

They all drank again to their agreement, and then St. Vrain and his friends left.

When they had gone through the door, Barlow looked over at White Bear, who had remained silent through Barlow's dealings with St. Vrain. "Ye think I done the right thing, hoss?" he asked.

"Yes, old chap. The men who plotted this are bloody enemies of your people. And in war, it's only right to destroy those bleedin' enemies however you can."

Barlow nodded. "Obliged, White Bear." He grinned. "Too bad they didn't ask you, too."

"I don't want anything to do with that bloody old thing, old chap," White Bear said with a chuckle. "They're your enemies, not mine, really."

"You're jist afeared of havin' to make a decision," Barlow said with a laugh.

"I think not, old chap," White Bear said sternly. Then he, too, laughed.

7

THE TRIAL WAS over in a matter of days. The deck was stacked against the rebels, and everyone—including the defendants—knew it. The verdict, of course, was known before the trial even started. After it was over, Barlow could see no real reason to argue with the decision. It was a sound one, as far as he was concerned, even if it was decided before it started.

The hanging of the rebels was not delayed for long, and the city began to return to some sort of normalcy. Barlow and White Bear had taken up with Rosaria and Inez as soon as they had gotten to town, and now that the trial and hanging were over, Barlow was free to simply lay back and relax. Or so he thought.

The day after the hanging, Lieutenant Prescott Johnston showed up with a small detachment at Viuda Garza's house, where Barlow and White Bear were again staying.

"Don't tell me," Barlow said when he greeted the young officer at the door, "Cap'n Newberry wants to see me and he cain't wait another minute. Right, hoss?"

"Yessir," Johnston said warily. "And I'd be obliged if

you were to come along without causin' trouble, Mister
Barlow."

"Trouble? I don't never cause no trouble, hoss," Barlow
said with a grin.

Johnston remembered the terrifying look he had seen
on Barlow's face the last time the old mountain man was
recalcitrant about being summoned to Captain Miles Newberry's office. It was not a pleasant sight, and Johnston
did not want to see it again. Or worse, have Barlow act
upon the anger that had put the look there.

"Are you comin' along, sir?" Johnston asked again.

"Well, now, hoss, I reckon that won't put me out none,"
Barlow allowed. "Jist let me git dressed."

"I'll be waiting," Johnston said. He was wary, wondering if Barlow was just going to go back inside and stay
there, leaving him and his men out in the cold.

But Barlow came out a few minutes later, accompanied
by Buffalo 2. White Bear had decided to stay behind,
reveling a little more in the pleasures afforded by Inez.

"Let's go, hoss," Barlow said jovially. He felt pretty
good, all things considered. Rosaria had left him gasping
with her lovemaking not long ago, the trial and hanging
were over with, and in maybe two or three months he
could begin looking for Anna again. That almost made
him sad, realizing that he had to wait yet some more. But
he had hope in his heart that his search would be over as
soon as he got to San Diego.

Captain Newberry looked surprised when Barlow
walked into his office. "I didn't expect you so soon," he
said, trying only a little to keep the sarcasm out of his
voice.

"I was in a charitable humor," Barlow said flatly, taking
a seat across the desk from the officer. Buffalo 2 plopped
down next to the chair, his great head on his big paws.
"So, Cap'n, jist why'd you call me here?"

"I need your services again, Mister Barlow," Newberry said. "I have a number of papers that must go to Bent's place up on the Arkansas. It's important that these papers get to Mister Bent as quickly as possible."

"Why not send a couple of your boys?" Barlow asked, his mood beginning to sour already.

"They're all needed here. Since that damn revolt, we've been busy as all hell here."

"What's so important about these papers that they have to get there right away? Besides, I thought Bent was dead."

"This is Charles's brother, Bill," Newberry said. "He was partners with Charles and St. Vrain. He runs their tradin' post up on the Arkansas. He was gonna come here soon's he heard about the revolt, but he was convinced to stay there just in case the rumor about the Mexican army returnin' was true."

Barlow decided not to argue anymore. He nodded. "You want I should leave now?" he asked.

Newberry's eyebrows rose in question. "No argument, Barlow?" he asked, surprised.

"Not this time, Cap'n. This Bill Bent just lost his brother in a most heinous way. If he needs these papers, I figure the least I can do is to get them to him as fast as I can."

Newberry was impressed. He had not expected it of a man like Barlow. "It might be best if you did. You can make it a fair piece to Raton Pass before dark sets in."

Barlow nodded again. "I'll go fetch my horse." He grimaced at the mention of it.

"You have a mule, don't you, Barlow?" Newberry asked. He remembered Barlow correcting him on that the last time he had an assignment for him.

"Did have. Ol' Beelzebub. He got hisself kilt down in the little battle we had on the way up here."

"That mule must've been something special," Newberry said, surprised again.

"I don't know about that, Cap'n. But I had him a long time. Since the mountain days. He was better'n any damn horse I ever had."

"You prefer mules, then?"

Barlow nodded.

Newberry dipped his pen in the inkwell on his desk and scratched something on a small piece of paper. "Take this to the wrangler," he said, handing Barlow the paper. "You can have your pick of our mules. I'm not sure you'll find one as good as that last one, but maybe you can get one close."

"Obliged, Cap'n," Barlow said. It was his turn to be surprised. He rose. "I best be on my way then. Soon's I git that mule and my few possibles, I'll be back." He hurried out, Buffalo 2 at his side. He rode the captured horse to the corral well away from the plaza. He gave the note to the soldier in charge there, and then wandered through the corral, checking out the few mules that were there. He found one that seemed to suit his needs. The animal was big and powerful looking, and appeared to be able to easily carry Barlow's bulk. The big, broad chest indicated stamina. The legs were solid and sturdy. The mule did not seem to mind Buffalo 2 sniffing around at his feet, trying to get his scent fixed.

Finally Barlow patted the big, gray-black beast on the neck. "Well, mule, looks like you're the new Beelzebub," he said, following his habit of keeping the same name for his animals. He got his saddle off the horse and put it on the mule, then bridled it. He pulled himself into the saddle and clucked for the mule to turn. A slight tap of his heels on the animal's sides was enough to get it moving.

At Viuda Garza's house, Barlow explained his new task to White Bear, who said he would go along. They gathered up their few belongings, and headed for the door. With a smile, Viuda Garza stopped them and gave them a satchel of tamales, a bag of tortillas and two clay jars, sealed with beeswax, full of cooked spicy beans that the two men could heat up over a fire.

"Muchas gracias," Barlow said. It would be much better than jerky and hardtack.

Outside, White Bear stopped, looking at Barlow's mount. "A new Beelzebub?" he asked, surprised.

Barlow grinned a little. "Yep. Army gave him to me."

White Bear nodded. He and Barlow mounted their riding animals and, with Buffalo 2 accompanying them, rode to Newberry's office. The Shoshoni waited outside while Barlow went in. He returned less than a minute later carrying a small leather pouch, which he slid into the possibles sack hanging from his saddle.

They rode into Bent's adobe fort a week later, and were introduced to the short, tough-looking owner.

Bent took the pouch quietly, then pointed to the small room on the second level. "You can cut your dry up there, amigos," he said. "Just don't overdo it. I got no fondness for drunken Injins runnin' around here."

"I'm not bloody fond of that either, old chap," White Bear said with an annoyed grimace.

Bent just nodded, not really paying attention. He turned absent-mindedly and went into his quarters.

As Barlow and White Bear left, the Shoshoni muttered, "Bloody stupid bastard. Bleedin' arse, talkin' about drunken Indians as if . . ."

Barlow stopped his friend. "Go easy on him, hoss," he said quietly. "Remember what jist happened to his brother. He's grievin', and not thinkin' real well, I figure."

White Bear glared at Barlow for a few moments, wondering whether his friend had suddenly turned against him. Then the sense of what Barlow had said filtered through to him. He breathed deeply and then nodded. "You're right, old chap."

They continued on up to the small bar. But no sooner had they downed one drink when Bent hurried in. "I'm sorry to impose on you, ol' chil'," he said to Barlow. "But I'll need you to get back down to Taos right away."

"That ain't funny, hoss," Barlow grumbled.

"It wasn't meant to be, Mister Barlow. There is information that must get down to Captain Newberry, or perhaps Colonel Price, with alacrity. The papers I received indicated that you would return as soon as I requested it of you. I am doing so."

"You really are serious, ain't you, hoss?" When Bent nodded, Barlow nodded. "We'll need somethin' to fill our meatbags with before we ride out. And somethin' better'n jerky and hard biscuits for the trail."

"The dinin' room's next to my quarters, along the other wall. Charlotte, the cook, is the best. She'll fill your meatbags well, and make sure you have some food to take. While you're feedin', I'll have some of my men tend your animals and make sure they're fed and watered."

Bent turned, took three steps, then spun back. "I am obliged to you, Mister Barlow. And to you, White Bear. I'm afraid I might've been a little curt, but my mind is on other matters."

Barlow and White Bear nodded and watched as Bent walked out. They finished another drink and then headed downstairs. It did not take long to find the dining room, and soon they were filling themselves on a delightful array of foods, many of which they had not tasted before. The large black woman also made sure that Buffalo 2 had a big plateful of food.

Finally sated, the two men relaxed to sip coffee and puff on their pipes.

Bent entered a few minutes later and handed Barlow the familiar-looking pouch. "I'm obliged, Mister Barlow," he said. "Your animals are ready and are out in front here. Charlotte has placed some vittles in your possibles sacks."

Barlow nodded. He stood and knocked the ashes out of his pipe into the fireplace and then slid it away. He led the way out, followed by Buffalo 2 and then White Bear. The two men mounted up, touched the brims of their hats in Bent's direction and trotted out through the wide double doors.

Half an hour later, Barlow belched mightily. "Damn," he said with a shake of the head, "I wish we could've taken our time with that meal. Them fixin's was damn good, but gobblin' 'em down like we did sure ain't sittin' well with this ol' chil'."

"I'm not suffering, old chap," White Bear said. "Maybe it isn't how bloody fast you ate but how much you stuffed into that bloody great gut of yours." He laughed.

Barlow scowled at the Shoshoni, but then laughed himself. "Could be you're right, hoss."

Like the trip to Bent's Fort, the journey back to Taos was uneventful, except for the freezing rain that fell throughout one afternoon where they could find no real shelter. Still, they made good time, and pulled into Taos late on the afternoon of the sixth day.

Barlow headed into Newberry's office, again leaving White Bear and Buffalo 2 outside. He handed the pouch to the captain. "Bent was in a mighty powerful hurry to get them papers to you, Cap'n," he said wearily.

"Sit, Mister Barlow," Newberry said.

Annoyed, Barlow did and sat quietly while Newberry sifted through the papers. Then the captain looked up at Barlow. "I'll need you to head down to Santa Fe right away, Mister Barlow," he said.

"Send somebody else, hoss. I've been on the trail more'n a week without stoppin' really. I ain't had but one meal in that time, and not even a decent drink."

"Colonel Price needs to see this information," Newberry said, his irritation growing.

Barlow was still more annoyed. "Like I said, hoss, send somebody else. You got enough old trappers and such fellers here. Anyone of 'em'd be more'n willin' to make the ride."

"But those men are not being paid by the Army. You are."

Barlow rubbed a hand across his face. "All right, Cap'n," he said. "But I ain't leavin' out till mornin'. I need a good night's sleep, and some robe time with some lusty *señorita*."

Newberry started to object, but Barlow stopped him before he really got started. "Besides, the mule needs rest and decent tendin'."

Newberry nodded. "I'll send a couple of men over to your place directly. They'll tend to your mule—and White Bear's horse, too, if he's goin' with you again. They'll see to it that they're fed, watered, curried and checked over. And they'll get them back to you before dawn."

"That'll suit me," Barlow said, rising. He headed out and explained the situation to White Bear as they rode toward Viuda Garza's. "You can come along again, or set out here for a spell, hoss," he said to the Shoshoni.

"I have nothing to do here, old chap, except . . ." He stopped and then grinned mightily. "Of course, there's Inez to occupy my time."

"True, hoss, but remember, Lupe is in Santa Fe, and it's been a while now since you've seen her."

"You do have a bloody good way of making a chap see the light of reason, old chap."

"I reckon it's a gift, hoss," Barlow said, just as they pulled up at the house.

They tied the animals off and went inside. Both were quite pleased to see that Rosaria and Inez were there, waiting for them in the single cramped room they shared.

8

OVER THE NEXT three weeks, Barlow and White Bear made one more trip to Bent's Fort and back, and three journeys between Taos and Santa Fe. They managed a night now and again with either Rosaria and Inez in Taos or Natividad and Lupe in Santa Fe. The constant traveling, always on the rush, was tedious and tiring—and grew more and more irritating with every mile they covered.

Finally White Bear had had enough. "You can make this next bloody jaunt to Santa Fe on your own, old chap," he told Barlow on the night before they were to leave Taos again. "I think I'll just stay right here and enjoy Inez's comforts."

Barlow shoved another tamale in his mouth and chewed. He could understand White Bear's reluctance to make the trip to Santa Fe again. Still, it would be a lonely, boring trip without his friend to break the monotony. "I don't reckon I can blame you none," he said after swallowing. He grinned halfheartedly. "Of course, Lupe's gonna be angrier'n a wet hornet when she finds out you ain't there with me."

"It's a bloody chance I'll have to take, old chap," White Bear answered with a small grin.

Barlow nodded. He and Buffalo 2 started out the next morning alone. A mile or so out of town, the Newfoundland stopped and looked back, confused. Barlow dismounted and knelt by the animal. "It's okay, Buffler," he said while stroking the dog's head. "White Bear's all right. He's jist stayin' behind this trip."

It didn't really stop the dog's confusion, but there was no more Barlow could do. He felt strange about it all, too. It was the first time in several years that he was making a trip of any length at all without his Shoshoni friend. It left him with an eerie feeling.

Making it worse was the fact that without White Bear along to keep him distracted, Barlow had too much time to think. And despite all his vows to not do it, he could not help but think of Anna. He wondered if she was all right, worried whether she might be sick, feared that she would forget him, or worse, might be dead. The long, lonely trip had him cursing the winter and his being stuck here when he should be out looking for his daughter.

He rode into Santa Fe late on the third day after having left Taos, and walked into Colonel Price's office minutes later. He tossed the pouch on the officer's desk and sank into a chair. Buffalo 2 flopped heavily on the floor with a big sigh.

Price read for a while, and then said, "You might be pleased to note, Mister Barlow, that a trip back to Taos is not required immediately."

"Well, hallelujah," Barlow said sarcastically. He rose. "You know where to find me. Jist make sure you don't try to do so for a spell. This ol' chil' needs some extra robe time."

Price nodded. "Where's your friend? That Shoshoni?"

"Had enough of travelin' for a spell and decided to stay

up there in Taos. Cain't say as I can fault him for sich."
He headed out and rode the short distance to the house
he usually shared with White Bear, Natividad and Lupe.
The women weren't there, which angered Barlow at first,
but then he realized it was probably for the best. He didn't
have the energy to take care of Natividad, nor the incli-
nation to have to explain to Lupe why White Bear was
not there.

He perfunctorily tended to the mule after unsaddling it,
then went inside. He flopped on the bed, pulled the blankets around him against the cold—the fire had not been
lit in days, he suspected—and fell asleep almost instantly.

He felt a lot better in the morning, but he was hungry.
He headed out and was about to hop on the mule to ride
to the cantina where Natividad and Lupe were usually to
be found, but then decided that Beelzebub needed even
more rest than he had needed. With rifle in hand, and
Buffalo 2 at his side, Barlow walked on. It wasn't really
very far, and the hunger pushed him to keep a good pace,
and he was there shortly.

As he had hoped, Natividad and Lupe were there. Natividad ran over and threw her arms around him before
kissing him hotly despite the place being fairly crowded.
He smiled at her and headed to a table, where he sat. "I'm
one hungry ol' chil', woman," he said in mock ferocity.
"Best git me some food *pronto*."

Natividad, who had perched herself on Barlow's lap as
soon as he sat, kissed him again and said enthusiastically,
"Sí!" She rose and hurried toward the kitchen in the rear.

Lupe stood there, looking forlorn. "Where ees *Señor*
White Bear?" she asked worriedly.

Barlow said nothing for a few moments. He realized he
just couldn't tell her that White Bear didn't want to make
the trip here again. That would only break the woman's
heart even more. "He's still up in Taos," he finally said

slowly. "The army up there asked him to go up to Bent's Fort to deliver some things," he lied smoothly. "He'll be here next time fer certain."

Lupe looked rather crushed.

"He said for me to tell you that he misses you very much and wishes he could be here," Barlow said, extending the lie.

The young Mexican woman smiled just a little and seemed to brighten a bit. She went off toward the kitchen. Barlow watched her. Lupe stopped and talked with Natividad, who patted her friend's shoulder. Soon after, Lupe slipped out the back door.

Natividad returned to the table with several bowls and plates of hot, spicy food that she set down in front of Barlow. "Whiskey?" she asked. "Or coffee, *mi corazón?*"

"Coffee fer now, *señorita bonita.*"

By the time she returned just minutes later, Barlow was well on his way to polishing off his meal. He ate with determination and purpose. Natividad was used to this by now, so was not surprised. She was, however, still a bit bemused by it. She had never seen a man put away food like this big American.

He eventually had enough. "Damn, woman, that plumb shined, it did." He pulled out his pipe, tamped it full of tobacco and lit it from the candle on the table. Then he sat back, puffing contentedly. After a bit of silence, he asked, "Can you git away from here, woman?"

"Now?" she asked.

"Yes, now."

"No," she said, face clouding over with sorrow. "I can't do so now."

Barlow smiled at her. "It's all right, woman," he said quietly. "You can come tonight, though?"

"*¡Sí! ¡Sí!*"

"*Bueno.*" Barlow rose, pulled on his coat and picked

up his rifle. "I'll be waitin' fer you, woman," he said. Then he kissed her and left.

He spent the day caring for Beelzebub, making sure the animal was all right despite his hard use over the past few weeks, napping some, and just relaxing, letting his muscles stretch and loosen after all the time in the saddle. He lit the fires and kept them going, with some coffee on to be available.

Barlow was well rested when Natividad arrived just after dark. She shivered a little when she pulled off her serape and tossed it aside. She moved into Barlow's strong, warm, comforting embrace. He just held her there a while, letting his heat flow into her, and just simply enjoying the feel of her against him.

She soon stirred, though, her arms wrapping around his big midsection, hugging him tight. She tilted up her head, eyes wanton, lips wanting. Barlow's huge neck bent, and his mouth covered hers, and their tongues parried and advanced. He managed to kick off his moccasins, and she pushed off her leather shoes.

Barlow was still surprised at the excitement and passion this woman raised in him. He scooped her up in his arms and carried her to the bedroom, which was warm now that the fire had had time to drive the chill away. Barlow set Natividad down on her feet. With big, clumsy fingers, he undid the buttons on her blouse and peeled it away, revealing her firm, ripe breasts, dusky in color with nipples and areolas so dark they were almost black.

He knelt and tugged her skirt down, revealing inch by inch her lower belly, and dark, moist womanhood, and then her long, perfectly shaped legs. He kissed her belly, tongued her navel, licked a trail down from belly button to the top of her womanly hair.

Natividad moaned softly as his lips began another feather-light trip across her belly. She grasped his unruly mop of hair and pressed his face against her flesh. Then she tugged his hair, pulling him up. Her lush, full lips were slightly parted, waiting for him. Her deep brown eyes were half closed, but still had a tremendous amount of magnetism for him, drawing him to her. He heeded their call. Pulling her into his arms, he kissed her hard, deep. The touch of her sweet tongue roared straight to his groin, leaving him as hard as a money lender's heart.

With lips locked, Natividad began working Barlow's shirt out of his pants and then tugging it up. They had to break their mouth clinch so that he could pull the shirt over his head and drop it to the floor. Then their mouths came together again, hungrily trying to devour each other.

Natividad finally pushed him away a little bit. She smiled hotly at Barlow, her eyes smoky with desire. She undid the buttons on his pants and tugged them down, kneeling as she did. He kicked himself free of the pants, but Natividad stayed where she was, as if studying Barlow's manhood, which was staring her in the face. Her tongue edged out and flicked the end of his lance ever so lightly.

Barlow gasped at the exquisiteness of that touch. He moaned when her lips parted and encircled his hardness, her mouth sliding as far as possible down its length and then retreating ever so slowly, tantalizingly.

Barlow reached for Natividad's hair, and a few pins jostled loose. Pulling away from him, Natividad looked up and smiled lasciviously. She finished pulling the pins out and her glossy black hair tumbled free, spilling over her delicate shoulders, and partly obscuring her breasts.

"Better, *mi corazón*?" she asked breathlessly.

"*Sí*, little one," he breathed, not sure he could really talk.

"*Bueno.*" She gently grasped his lance and lifted it a little, then ran her tongue down the shaft, from scrotum to tip.

Barlow quivered. The feeling was more than heavenly. It was beyond anything he had ever experienced. He did not know how much longer he could stand there without reaching a climax with what she was doing to him. At the same time, he wanted it to go on forever and beyond. It was a most delicious feeling.

But he wanted her, too. With some reluctance, he pulled her gently up and kissed her. "Another time you can do that, if you desire, little one," he breathed into her ear.

"Oh, *sí*, I want that," she responded. "What would you like to do, *mi corazón*?"

"Everything," he responded honestly. "All at once."

"That would be *muy bueno*," Natividad said ardently. She turned to face the bed, her back to him. She bent at the waist, placing her hands on the bed, spreading her legs just a little. She looked teasingly back over her shoulder. "How about thees, eh? You like thees?"

"Goddamn yes," Barlow said through constricted throat, as he gazed at her perfectly formed buttocks, her womanhood just peeking out, enticing him, beckoning to him, begging for him.

He stepped up, taking his rock-solid shaft in his hand and then tenderly introduced it to her receptive sheath. She sucked in a deep breath as he slid deeper and deeper into her. She shook as a small climax came over her, surprising her a little with the quickness with which it had arrived.

Barlow, too, drew in air with a sharp hiss, as pleasure raced through his genitals to explode in his brain and then rain down through the rest of his body. He did not want to move. Ever. He wanted to stay there like that until the end of time, his incredibly hard shaft deeply immersed in her silken passageway.

But his body called for him to move, and Natividad herself was slowly, gently rotating her buttocks, wanting more of him. With eyes closed, he drew back and plunged into her again and again, strongly, steadily, smoothly. He grabbed her wide, beautiful hips and pounded into her with increasingly powerful thrusts.

Natividad screamed and shook as a climax washed over her like floodwater over a riverbank. She thought she might drown in it, but the thrill was so intense that she did not care right then if she died.

Moments later, Barlow roared like a grizzly on the prowl and rammed himself in and out of her so hard that somewhere among the swirling pleasures that clouded his brain, he thought he might hurt her. But she sure didn't seem to mind.

Drained, Barlow pulled himself out and then flopped on the bed, breathing heavily. Natividad climbed over him to the inside of the bed near the wall. She rested her head on his shoulder, too winded to speak, and placed a hand on his heaving chest.

"*Magnifico!*" she finally whispered.

"*Sí,*" he managed to gasp.

As her breathing returned to almost normal, Natividad reached out and pulled the blankets up over them. She nestled into the haven of his arms. Before long, they were both asleep.

They awoke in the same positions, virtually at the same time, and smiled at each other. Natividad rose and wrapped a blanket around her, tucking the ends into each other just above her breasts so it would not fall. She went and got coffee for Barlow and then made breakfast.

They partially dressed to eat at the table in the kitchen, and then Natividad tugged Barlow back into the bedroom, where she lovingly, joyfully finished the job she had started the night before. The feeling was so powerful that he hurt his neck from bunching up the muscles there and in his shoulders in the moments before exploding with the

most extraordinary climax he had ever had. It left him
almost weak, and certainly drained.

Barlow and Natividad spent the next three days in the
little house, making love, eating, sleeping, enjoying each
other's company. Then a soldier arrived to get him.

"Colonel Price needs you to make another trip to Taos,"
the soldier said almost apologetically.

Barlow nodded. He knew it was inevitable, and the past
three days had been magnificent. He wasn't sure he had
it in him to spend more time with Natividad anyway. She
plumb wore him out.

"Tell the colonel I'll be along directly," he said and
shut the door. Natividad was smiling at him, her eyes lusty
again. He grinned, too, and decided that he just might
have a little more in reserve.

9

BARLOW DROPPED OFF the pouch of dispatches with Captain Newberry and then rode straight on over to Viuda Garza's, where he found White Bear and Inez happily ensconced in the room. Rosaria was not around, which was just as well for the time being, Barlow thought. "How's doin's, hoss?"

"Quite well, old chap," White Bear said with a grin. "Inez has been most accommodating and Widow Garza has kept me bloody well fed. How about you, mate?"

"I got a few days rest down in Santa Fe this time, which helped considerable. Well, I got a few days off the trail," he added with a grin. "Cain't say as I rested a whole heap."

"Indeed," White Bear offered, eyebrows raised.

"Let's head to a cantina, hoss. I got me a big thirst, and since it's so late in the day, I'd hate for Widow Garza to have to make me up somethin' to fill my meatbag."

"Right-o, old chap. Be with you very soon."

Barlow shook his head in bemusement, and headed toward the kitchen.

Viuda Garza was there and she gave him a cup of coffee. "Are you hungry?" she asked.

"Plenty hungry. But me'n White Bear will be headin' to one of the cantinas to sup. You should be asleep soon, ma'am."

The old lady smiled and nodded. Barlow was still not sure how much of his talk she understood, but she did seem to be grasping more of what he said. Or at least pretending well.

Barlow gulped down the coffee when White Bear came out of the room with Inez. The three left into another windy, snowy storm. Inez left them at the plaza, heading toward her home, Barlow assumed. Soon after, Barlow and White Bear were in a cantina, their coats off, and a surly young Mexican man was bringing them food and whiskey.

As they ate, Barlow said, "That Lupe sure misses you, hoss. She was pinin' for you. I got no idear why, but she was."

White Bear grinned and nodded. "Nice to know someone thinks bloody highly of me, old chap."

They ate in silence for a bit, then White Bear asked, "Something eating at you, old chap?"

"Nah. What makes you think that, hoss?"

White Bear shrugged. "We've been together several bloody years now, old chap, in the worst of situations and in the bleedin' best of them, too. I've come to know you pretty bloody well by now. I know something's stuck in your craw. So out with it, mate."

"You know, hoss, you can be a most annoyin' critter at times." He sighed, took another bite, sighed again, then said, "If I had known we—or at least I—was gonna do so much travelin' around durin' the winter, I would've jist headed out for San Diego again." His anger grew as the thought expanded. "Hell, I could've had Anna by now and been halfway back to Oregon country."

"You're probably right, old chap. But there's not bloody much can be done about it now. Stop your fretting."

"I cain't, goddammit," Barlow snapped, angrily chomping on a tortilla wrapped around some kind of meat and beans. "I had too much time to think about such booshwa on the way back from Santa Fe. It's plaguin' my heart that I cain't jist go git her. There's always somethin' standin' in my way. I worry that the more time that goes by, the worse off my chances are of ever findin' Anna."

"We'll find her, old chap. And bloody soon, too."

"I hope you're right, goddammit."

Barlow spent the next few days with Rosaria, White Bear and Inez, enjoying himself, but missing Natividad, and feeling the need to look for Anna again growing inside him.

When Captain Newberry sent for him to make another trip to Taos, Barlow went to White Bear and bluntly told him, "You're makin' this trip, hoss. I'll be damned if I'll go back down there and try to make up another lie about you to tell poor Lupe."

White Bear was about to retort when he stopped, then nodded. He knew there was more to it than just having to tell some story to a woman. He reasoned that Barlow did not want to ride that trail alone again, giving him too much more time to think—and thus fall into melancholy—about the situation with Anna.

"Sure, old chap," he said. "I'm getting bloody tired of such cramped quarters here anyway."

They pulled out the next morning. Barlow was relieved to have his Shoshoni friend along. The Indian had a way of keeping his mind off of matters that plagued him, like not being able to find his daughter. It made the travel ever

so much easier on him when he did not have to wallow
in his self-induced melancholy.

In Santa Fe once more, they had a jolly reunion with
Natividad and Lupe. The latter woman clung to White
Bear, almost never letting go of him, much to the Sho-
shoni's annoyance and Barlow's amusement.

A couple of days later, Barlow and White Bear headed
for their favorite cantina. When their eyes had adjusted to
the gloomy interior, they spotted Manuel Ortega sitting
alone at a table.

"¡Hola, amigos!" the Mexican shouted. He waved
them over to his table.

"How's doin's, hoss?" Barlow said as he and White
Bear took seats. Buffalo 2 went to check out Ortega with
his nose and was rewarded with a few friendly pats on
the head. The dog, satisfied at knowing this man, went
back and lay down next to Barlow's chair.

Glasses for the two new arrivals were brought, and Ortega poured them some wine.

"So, hoss," Barlow started after a sip, "what've you
been up to lately?"

"Following your advice, *señor*," Ortega said with a
grin. "When the trouble started up in Taos, I took off up
into the hills and stayed there until things quieted down."

"Wise of you, old chap."

Ortega nodded. "I didn't want anything to do with those
doings. I might be proud of Mexico and wish this land
still belonged to it, but I could see that my people had no
chance of overcoming the *americanos*. Even with the help
of the Taos Indians. All those *babosos* did was to bring
more trouble on our people."

Ortega stopped for a deep draught of wine. "After that
loco business in Taos ended, I slipped out of the mountains and headed down here. I've been staying out of the
way of the *americanos*, just to be certain, but the *soldados*

don't seem to be bothering us Mexicans overly much."

Barlow and White Bear nodded. "I still think it was the best thing for you, hoss," Barlow said.

"It was. But like I said before, *señores*, I don't have to like it that the *americanos* have taken over my country."

The two newcomers nodded again. There was nothing they could really say to that. Neither had had his land taken away from his people.

"So, *mis amigos*, what have you been up to since the trouble?" Ortega asked.

"We was here when we got word of it," Barlow said. "Me and White Bear joined up with St. Vrain and his men for the march up there. Had us a rousin' fight with some of those insurrectionists on the way, but by the time we rode into Taos, them doin's was about over. 'Cept for the Army blastin' the hell out of the pueblo."

He stopped to light his pipe. "Since then, we've been riding the trail almost constantly 'tween here and Taos. Made a couple trips up to Bent's place up on the Arkansas. I ain't had more'n a day or two in any one place since the revolt."

Barlow grimaced at the thought of all the traveling. "Like I said to White Bear jist the other day, if I knew I'd be doin' this much travelin' about in the winter weather, I'd have jist taken off for San Diego to start. I could've had Anna safe in my arms by now."

Ortega sat deep in thought. Then he said quietly, "Why don't you just go now, *amigo*?"

"Crossin' them mountains in the winter'd likely put us under, hoss," Barlow replied. "You know that. It's why I was havin' to wait out the winter here. I didn't expect to be ridin' back and forth all the time. But at least I know these parts a little bit now. Them mountains out there are new to me, hoss."

The Mexican looked around, to make sure no one else

was listening, then said, "There is another way, *señores*. It's much easier at this time of year."

Barlow and White Bear looked at Ortega in surprise.

"It is to the south, *amigos*," Ortega said. "That way the mountains are not so tall or so formidable, and there is much desert. The desert continues to the west, all the way to the ocean, I think. At this time of year, traveling should be fairly easy and comfortable."

"Why didn't you tell us this when we left here last year with General Kearny?" Barlow demanded, a touch of anger in his voice.

Ortega shrugged and smiled a little. "The general had just taken over my country, *señores*," he said. "I was not going to help him, or his army." He sighed and took in some more wine. "I also thought that since you were going there with the *americano* army, that you would stay there and find your daughter. I did not know you would be coming back here."

"It weren't my choice, hoss," Barlow growled. "That son of a bitch Kearny sent me back this way before I even got to San Diego."

"So I understood, *amigo*."

"Why didn't you tell us this when we met you up in Taos a few weeks before the bloody revolt?" White Bear asked.

"Yeah, hoss," Barlow tossed in.

Ortega shrugged. "I didn't know how things would turn out, *amigos*. I took a great chance in telling you about the talk of rebelling. That was enough danger for me at one time."

Barlow accepted that. He didn't like it, but he accepted it. "You wouldn't help Kearny, but you don't mind helping us?" Barlow asked after his annoyance had subsided.

"No," Ortega said simply. "You are not really soldiers, *señores*. You are . . . friends." He seemed afraid that his two companions would laugh at him, or denounce him for such presumptuousness. "You two have always treated me well, like an equal, which many—most—*americanos* don't do. *Señor* Robidoux did not. I don't mind helping men who have become friends."

Barlow nodded. He could understand that. He thought he could also understand why the Mexican had been reluctant to tell him about this other way to San Diego. He could not have known which way things were going to go, what with all the rumors that had been floating about. "Where is this easier route?" he asked.

Ortega pulled out a piece of well-tanned buckskin from a sack he had on the floor and a somewhat sharpened piece of wood. He held the wood over the candle flame until it was burnt a little. Then, using the charcoal on the point, he began drawing a crude map of the way he thought Barlow and White Bear should go.

When Ortega was done, he turned it and slid it across the table so Barlow and White Bear could look at it. But, since neither the former mountain man nor his Shoshoni companion had ever been even remotely near any of these places, they stared blankly at the map.

"I cain't make head nor tails of sich places, hoss," Barlow finally said. "That whole thing's little more than gibberish to me. Might's well write us a guidebook all in Spanish for all the good it'll do us."

"Ah, *señores*," Ortega said, "you are men of the wilderness. You have traveled many miles of country, much of it unknown to you. Yet you have always found your way, *señores*. You can do this, too."

Barlow didn't know why, but he was still unsure of himself. With a sideways glance at White Bear, he could see that the Shoshoni was feeling the same. He sat there thinking, and soon realized that he was worried that he would somehow get lost and never find Anna. It was, he told himself silently, a foolish thought, but it was there nonetheless.

After a few more sips and a refill of wine, Barlow suddenly had an idea. "Why don't you come with us, hoss?" he asked. "You can show us the way, sort of as a guide." He was warming to the idea. "Not only do you know the way and the areas we'll have to go through, but you can probably smooth our passage if we come across any other Mexican settlements. And most important, you can interpret for me when we git to San Diego. I've learned some Spanish from Natividad while I've been here, but I really don't know more'n a few words of it. Certainly not enough to get by. You helped out a heap when we was questioning folks hereabouts last summer."

"I don't think I could do that, *señores*," Ortega said.

"Can't do it, hoss?" Barlow demanded. "Or don't want to do it? Are you sendin' us out into hostile territory to git our hair lifted? Maybe you really do hate all Americans, not just soldiers, and figure this is a way of gittin' rid of a couple of devilish gringos."

"No, *señor*!" Ortega said sharply. "That is not it!"

"Then what's keepin' you from comin' along with us?" Barlow's eyes burned with fire.

Ortega thought about it for a few moments, but he could see no reason why he shouldn't go. Life in Taos and Santa Fe would never be the same after the American takeover, and the failed revolt. He thought San Diego might be as good a place as any for a footloose Mexican to spend some time. He did not want to work for Robidoux anymore, not after he had seen what the Frenchman's operation had done with the children. Besides, now that the Utes had run Robidoux out of his trading post, he didn't want to have to go searching. The thought of getting out of the harsh winter weather for a while sealed it.

"All right, *señores*," he said, brightening. "I will go with you. But you must buy me supplies and things. I don't have the pesos for that."

"Sounds fair to me, hoss," Barlow said, relaxing considerably. "What do you think, White Bear?"

"I think we can trust this bloody white-eyed devil." He burst into a wide grin at the look of terror that had flashed across Ortega's face.

"When do we leave, *amigos*?" Ortega asked, realizing that the Shoshoni had only been joking.

"Day after tomorrow?" Barlow suggested.

White Bear and Ortega agreed. Each raised his glass, and they drank deeply of the wine to seal their pact.

10

THE THREE MEN spent the next few days gathering supplies and looking for a couple of pack mules. But by now their money was low, and mules—as well as horses—were out of their range.

"So what do we do?" Barlow asked that night as they sat in a cantina drinking whiskey.

"I suppose we could find some isolated rancho and bloody ride away with a couple, old chap."

"I ain't much given to stealin' horses, or mules, hoss," Barlow said. "Sich doin's might bring honors amongst your people, you red-skinned devil, but around here, hoss, it'll git us hanged, as you should know from your time back in the Settlements."

"Have you gotten scared in your old age, you bleedin' white-eyed demon?"

"Hell," Barlow spit.

"Well, if that won't work, old chap, why don't you ask Colonel Price for a couple of mules or horses."

"I don't reckon he'll be so freehanded with horseflesh," Barlow said, rubbing a hand across his stubbled chin.

"Maybe he will," Ortega chimed in. "The army has taken many horses from the people here and in Taos. He can't use them all."

"Hell, he'll find some use for 'em, hoss." Barlow sat in thought, then slowly grinned a little. "But I got me an idear of where we might jist git some." He polished off his drink and rose, tugging on his blanket coat. "I'll be back directly, boys. Mayhap even with a couple of mules." With Buffalo 2 at his side, he marched out.

Minutes later, he entered Ceran St. Vrain's store. It was warm and filled with smells familiar to Barlow—leather, fur of various kinds, the metal of traps, tobacco. "Mister St. Vrain here, hoss?" he asked the clerk working at the counter.

"He's in back. You want me to get him?"

"I'd be obliged." He strolled around the store for a few minutes, looking at all the wide variety of items, most of which he had little need for.

"*Monsieur* Barlow," St. Vrain said from a few feet behind Barlow. When Barlow turned to face him, he asked, "What can I do for you, *mon ami*?"

"I need a couple of pack mules, hoss."

"I can supply zem. *Bien sur!* And at a good price, *mon ami*." He was his usual ebullient self.

"Well, hoss, there's where we run into a wee problem. Me and my *amigos* are about out of pesos, most of which you already have, hoss, from all them supplies we bought."

"And you expect me to just give you ze mules?"

"I'd be mighty obliged if'n you was to do so."

St. Vrain spat out a few mouthfuls of French, none of which Barlow could understand, but he figured it was not complimentary to him. Finally the Frenchman ground to a halt. "You are *très fou, monsieur*," he said. "Very crazy."

"Mayhap, hoss, but I reckon it's the least you can do for me."

"And 'ow do you think zat?" St. Vrain demanded.

"Well, I was with you on that little jaunt up to Taos. But moreover, I was on the jury that took care of the critters who started that whole ruckus."

"Many men were on zat expedition, *monsieur*. And I could 'ave 'ad any number on ze jury."

"I reckon that's so, hoss, but why did you ask me?"

"I t'ought you could be trusted. Maybe I was wrong, eh?"

"Like hell. You knew damn well you could trust me to do what was needed. You had many a feller there you could've asked, men you've known for a long time. But you came to me. I ain't rightly sure why, but you did."

"Zat is true," St. Vrain admitted. He still didn't seem all that convinced, but Barlow had been a considerable help in that battle, and had spent plenty of pesos in his store. And he remembered why Barlow had bought all those supplies—to leave Santa Fe and head to San Diego to look for his daughter. He sighed. "All right, *monsieur*. But only two mules. No more."

"I am obliged, Mister St. Vrain," Barlow said solemnly. "Your help means a great deal to me, and I ain't ever gonna forget it. Mayhap I'll never be able to repay you your kindness, but if there's ever any way I can and you can get ahold of me, I'll do it."

St. Vrain nodded, suddenly feeling better. He was a good businessman, but he was also a jolly fellow, not prone to melancholy very often. And he liked people. Two mules would not set him back much.

•   •   •

Natividad was not happy with Barlow's leaving. Not happy at all. She considered telling him exactly how unhappy she was. But she was having trouble maintaining her anger as Barlow's hands, lips, and mouth played just the right notes on the instrument that was her body. Soon she melted into the passion he stoked in her.

And when they were done, she was so immersed in dreamy good feelings and warmth that she could not bring herself to yell at him. Still, she was now sad that he was leaving.

He said good-bye to her the next morning in a most delicious way, and then headed outside to saddle his mule. White Bear was already outside. He was again dressed as a Shoshoni—buckskin shirt, leggings and moccasins, the last with fur inside, as Barlow's were. He wore a blanket breechcloth and a long Whitney blanket coat. His pony was ready, and he was leaning back against the wall of the house, enjoying the sun, which was incredibly bright, but brought little in the way of real heat.

Barlow hurriedly saddled the mule, and he and White Bear mounted up. Buffalo 2, sensing that adventure was in the offing, pranced out ahead of the two mounted men. Barlow glanced back at the house and waved when he saw Natividad watching him. He thought he saw tears on her face, but he couldn't be sure. He and White Bear rode off.

Within minutes they were at St. Vrain's store. Manuel Ortega waited outside, his own horse saddled and ready. The three went inside, where St. Vrain greeted then with a hearty *"Bonjour, mes amis."*

"Hola," Ortega said, as Barlow and White Bear simply nodded.

"Your mules, zey are packed, *monsieur*," St. Vrain said. "I took ze liberty of having some of my men do zat."

"Much obliged, hoss," Barlow said, almost embarrassed.

St. Vrain nodded. "You boys, you 'ave a safe trip, eh? And a successful one."

"I sure hope it turns out that way, hoss," Barlow said solemnly. With White Bear, Ortega and Buffalo 2, he went outside and around to the back, where there was a small yard. There stood three mules. Barlow stopped short. "That son of a bitch," he breathed.

"Something wrong, *amigo*?" Ortega asked.

"I asked that ol' hoss in there for two mules. He gave me a hard time fer a spell about it, then gave it. Now there's three mules all loaded up. I'll be damned." He paused and turned. "I best go in and thank him for his generosity."

"I don't think that's wise, old chap," White Bear said. "If he had wanted your bloody thanks, he would've come out here with us."

Barlow pondered that for a moment, then nodded. "I reckon you're right, hoss," he allowed. "Well, boys, we best make tracks. Manuel, you take the lead, since you know where you're goin'. I suppose I'll ride the middle with the pack animals. That leaves you, White Bear, to watch our backs."

The two other men nodded, and they mounted their riding animals. They were almost out of the city when several soldiers raced up, calling them. They stopped and waited. The soldiers pulled to a stop. "Sorry to delay you men, but Colonel Price wanted me to give this to you, Mister Barlow." He held out a familiar-looking packet. "The colonel asks that you deliver these dispatches to General Kearny when you get to San Diego."

Barlow took the pouch and slipped it into the possible bag hanging from his saddle. "Reckon that won't put me out none," he allowed.

The sergeant leading the little patrol saluted. Then he and his men turned and galloped back the way they had come.

Barlow shook his head. "Damn, I thought we was gonna git clean out of here without havin' to do this." Then he grinned.

"You can just toss them to the winds once we move on, old chap," White Bear suggested.

Barlow shrugged. "What the hell, I'm goin' to San Diego anyway. Won't be no harm in makin' a quick stop to hand Kearny a sack of papers. Besides, hoss, it'll mean more pay, which we can use once we get out there."

"Always thinking, aren't you, old chap?" White Bear said with a smile.

"That's true. Now, let's ride. We're wastin' daylight."

By the time they hit the trail the next morning, they could see the differences in the countryside. From the ponderosa pine and scrub oak in Santa Fe and north, they now moved into a drier area. There was more piñon here, and some willows. The closer they got to Albuquerque, the more sage and yucca they saw. There was no snow on the ground really, except in the nooks and crannies of rocks. They ate well, however, not having to travel far off the road to hunt prairie chicken, antelope and wild turkeys.

The traveling was relatively easy, as the road was well defined. "My people, and the Spanish before us, have been using this trail for centuries," Ortega told his two companions the second night out. "*El Camino Real*—the King's Road—goes from Santa Fe all the way down to Chihuahua. And some say it goes on even to Mexico City."

"Well, all I can say is, hoss, that I'm grateful to them folks for doing so, since this here road makes our journey some easier," Barlow noted.

The next afternoon, they arrived in Albuquerque. It was a place much like Santa Fe, though considerably smaller. It sat on the high desert, keeping the temperatures low, though not as bad as in Taos. Still, there was little snow on the ground, since the area was so dry.

They did not stay but the one night. They were still too fresh on the trail to need to rest the animals, and Barlow was eager to be on the move again. They simply ate and had a few whiskeys in a cantina, and they slept in a stall at the livery stable, not wanting to waste the money for a room.

. The small group pulled out the next morning under a startlingly bright sky, its blue spreading as far as one could see in all directions. Not even a single cloud broke the azure expanse. The temperature was low, but bearable. While the sun stayed bright in the sky, it never did warm the day up much.

The road widened here, with the high, sparsely foliaged desert running off for miles in all directions. It made riding abreast possible, and they did so, though they were generally silent. Only Manuel Ortega was prone to gabbing for no real reason, but he kept his silence in deference to his two companions.

The Rio Bravo ran sluggishly to their right, as the road hugged the river's path. The Rio Bravo was rather small here, which surprised Barlow and White Bear, who only this past summer had traveled near its headwaters far to the north and west. Miles to the east and south, the faint blobs of mountains were visible in the crystal clear air.

They picked up speed a little now that they were on the relative flatness of the high desert, making twenty, sometimes even thirty miles a day.

"You sure you know where you're goin', hoss?" Barlow asked Ortega on their second night out from Albuquerque. This was, to his thinking, as bad as traveling across the Great Plains. There was nothing to really set your sights on as the land undulated along. Even with the well-defined road, Barlow didn't like traveling in this kind of country. He preferred the mountains, where, even if you ran into an impassable canyon or some other natural obstacle, a man didn't feel as small as a fly on a horse's back—lost and not sure where to go.

"*Sí,*" Ortega said. He glanced at Barlow and almost smiled. The big man truly seemed concerned. "Of course," he added, a smile tugging at his thin lips, "if you have a better way to go, *señor*, I will follow you."

"I don't reckon that'll be necessary," Barlow replied. "I jist wanted to make sure you knew where we was at and where we're goin'."

"Afraid, old chap?" White Bear asked, grinning.

Barlow gave the Shoshoni a withering glance. "Not in the least, hoss, but travelin' open country like this irritates me no end. There's somethin' unnatural about it."

"You did it back when you were a bloody mountain man," White Bear said. "From what you've told me, you crossed the bloomin' Plains from the Settlements to the mountains more than once."

"Didn't much like it then, neither," Barlow said matter-of-factly. "I was raised where there was trees and sich," he added. "Real trees, like up in the mountains, not them goddamn puny little things you got up there where you call home, hoss."

"I think you just like to bloody complain, mate," White Bear said, still grinning.

Barlow gave his friend another withering look, but then burst into laughter. "Reckon you jist might be right on that, hoss," he said. "I figure one of us has to complain, so it might's well be me."

"To tell you the bloody truth, old chap," White Bear said sarcastically, "I can see no bloody call for anyone to complain. We've had no bloomin' trouble on this trip, the traveling has been easy, and we've filled our meatbags regularly and well."

"Ain't we touchy all of a sudden," Barlow said. Then both he and White Bear laughed.

Ortega sat there shaking his head. He had never seen a more unlikely pair than these two men, but they got along so well that it seemed they had been brought together because they did so, despite their many differences. It both amused and bemused the Mexican.

11

A FEW DAYS later, they had just woken up for the day and were going about their morning ablutions and chores when all three men stopped and looked warily around. Buffalo 2 whined and looked confused, head cocked first one way, then the other.

"What'n hell's that?" Barlow asked in a whisper, trying to determine where the low, powerful rumbling sound was coming from. It seemed to be bubbling up from deep in the bowels of the earth under their feet, but that didn't seem to make sense to him.

"I'm not sure, old chap, but you can be bloody sure it's not another one of those bleedin' avalanches," White Bear said. He was baffled by the sound, and by the uneasiness that seemed to have settled over their camp, as if brought by the wind and deposited here.

"A buffler herd?" Barlow wondered out loud.

"There are no buffalo here, *señor*," Ortega offered. "Not so many as to make such a *muy grande* noise."

Then the rumble stopped as suddenly as it had started. The three men looked at each other for a few moments, then shrugged. As White Bear and Ortega went back to their tasks, Barlow glanced at the Newfoundland. The big dog was still acting strangely, as if he could sense something that the men couldn't. It bothered Barlow, since he knew the dog was not prone to behaving like this without just cause. But Barlow could not for the life of him figure out what was bothering the dog. With a nervous sigh, Barlow returned to cooking up the bacon and beans that were on the fire.

Soon after, they were sitting with their tin plates of food and tin mugs of coffee, eating and sipping, talking about the strange sound they had heard not long ago, and trying to come up with possible causes. But none had ever experienced anything like that before, so they came to no conclusions.

"Maybe it was just in our bloody imaginations," White Bear finally offered.

"All three of us?" Barlow asked in disdain. "An ol' hoss like you might have visions that include queersome noises with 'em, but this chil' certainly don't. And I reckon ol' Manuel don't either."

"That is true, *señores*," Ortega said. "I don't have no visions like that. Not when I haven't had nothing to drink." He grinned widely.

"Well, then, mates, maybe we just *thought* we bloody heard something."

"That don't make no more sense than thinkin' we made it up, hoss," Barlow said flatly. He started laughing, and it got harder and harder, until he had to wipe the tears of joy from his eyes.

All the while, his two companions looked at him as if he had just lost his reason. Even Buffalo 2 was peering strangely at his master, confused by this oddness in the man.

Finally Barlow slowed down enough to be able to speak

in fits and starts. "I jist had the thought . . . ," he gasped, ". . . jist thought that maybe it was . . ." He broke into more gales of laughter, shaking with it. He willed himself to stop. "I was jist thinkin' that maybe Mother Earth here . . ." He had to pause. "Maybe Mother Earth here had to relive herself of internal wind."

"The earth breaking wind?" White Bear said stupidly. "You think the earth was breaking wind?" The ludicrousness of it suddenly caught up to him, and he, too, began laughing, until he eventually had to hold his sides, which were hurting from the effort.

"Madre de dios," Ortega exclaimed. "That is funny, *amigo.*" He was soon also lost in the gales of mirth.

Buffalo 2 simply looked at all three men as if they had gone completely mad. He backed off a little and let out a small growl, preparing to defend himself from these friends-turned-lunatics.

It took some time, but the three companions finally stopped laughing. At least for the most part. Chuckles still erupted from any or all of the three on occasion for a while longer.

At last, Barlow said, "We best git movin' here, boys. We've wasted a heap of time on all this frivolity."

"Bloody crab," White Bear muttered even as he rose and headed toward the supplies to start packing the animals.

Ortega joined him, while Barlow cleaned up their things around the fire, "washing" their plates and pots with sand. In half an hour, they were done and ready to leave. But just as they began to pull themselves into their saddles, the rumbling began again. Once more they all looked at each other, wondering.

The growling noise grew stronger, louder, more insistent. Then the ground began to shake under their feet, seemingly rising and falling, rolling.

"Good Lord Almighty!" Barlow shouted as Beelzebub jerked at the reins. The mule's nostrils were widely flared and his eyes revealed his terror. He began shuffling and braying wildly, and Barlow had to use all his mighty strength to keep the animal from bolting.

"What the bloody 'ell!" White Bear exclaimed. He was on his pony, which pranced around, frightened but not yet ready to run off.

"*¡Madre de dios!*" Ortega spat out. He frantically made the sign of the cross on himself over and over, while trying to hold his skittish horse with his other hand.

One of the pack mules broke free from the bush to which it had been tied and raced across the buckling, heaving land.

"Dammit!" Barlow shouted as he watched the pack animal flee. He could not even quiet Beelzebub down enough to get into the saddle to chase the running beast. It was all he could do to keep the mule from bolting, too.

Buffalo 2 ran back and forth, barking, growling, unsure of what to do.

The ground began to crack and split, though not right where the men were. Still, they were awed all over again at what was happening all around them. There was nothing they could do: no way to outrun this thing—whatever it was—nowhere to go to escape it; nothing to do to stop it, or even lessen its destructiveness.

"*¡Terremoto!*" Ortega screamed as the earth roared with its disruption. "Earthquake!"

Barlow's eyes widened as he struggled to retain hold of the mule. He had heard of earthquakes, but he had never experienced one. He had heard some men talking about riding one out a long time ago during his mountain days, but he had been disinclined to put the story down as too much exaggeration. *The ground opening up and swallowing men, animals, lodges?* The thought was ridiculous. At least that's what he had thought until now. He had suddenly become a believer in such things.

The rumbling noise and the disconcerting shifting of the earth under their feet seemed to go on for hours, though it was really less than a minute. Then, as suddenly as it began, it stopped. An ominous silence descended, as even the horses and mules began to quiet down.

"Jesus, if that ain't the queersomest thing this chil's ever been through," Barlow said, still rather astonished at the experience he had just had. "Goddamn, that was some now."

White Bear wiped a hand across his sweating forehead. "That was bloody evil," he growled. "Bloody goddamn evil."

Ortega said nothing. He just rested his forehead against his horse's neck, and silently said a few prayers. He remained there for a while even after Barlow and White Bear had gone around trying to calm the horses and mules. It took them nearly an hour before the animals were settled enough to be trusted underneath them.

Barlow mounted Beelzebub. "You boys can stay here, if you like. I'm goin' out after that mule that took off. Maybe I can catch it before too long."

"Listen here, you bloody stupid bastard," White Bear snapped. "I am not staying in this bloody goddamn place. Not after that bloody earthquake. I don't know about Manuel, old chap, but I aim to ride south this very minute and put as much distance as I can between me and this bloody evil place."

"I ain't staying here by myself, *señores*," Ortega said hastily. "This place must house a *brujo* under the earth." He was decidedly nervous.

"*Brujo?*" Barlow asked. "What in hell's that?"

"A sorcerer," Ortega said tensely. "Like an evil spirit, *señor*."

White Bear nodded. "My Shoshoni blood tells me this is an evil place," he added. "Bad spirits live here. My medicine is not good in such a place." He, too, was growing agitated with anxiety.

"All right, boys," Barlow said. "Head on south. I'll catch up to you soon's I can. Jist don't put too many miles 'twixt here and you boys." He could understand their reluctance to stay around this place after what had just happened. It was the same reason he had been the first to mention going after the lost mule. That would get him away from the spot if the other two had decided to linger.

Barlow turned Beelzebub. "C'mon, Buffler," he said, as he trotted out of the devastated campsite, heading southeast. He didn't look back, but he knew that White Bear and Ortega were already riding off down the Camino Real, distancing themselves from the hellish site.

It took Barlow far longer than he had thought it would to find the mule. He almost gave up several times, but each time decided that just a little farther wouldn't hurt. He finally spotted the animal placidly cropping at the almost nonexistent grass down a slight rise. It was amid a large herd of antelope.

Barlow rode up to the mule from the downwind side, not alerting it, but the much more skittish antelope watched him warily, ready to take off in an instant, using their incredible speed to escape. Barlow finally grabbed the rope to the pack mule. Tugging it, he rode off. The animal followed without resistance.

As Barlow rode southwest, he realized he was out in the middle of all this open land, with nothing to really use as a landmark. While looking for the mule, he had not really paid all that much attention to where he was, so much was he concentrating on trying to spot the animal. He suddenly hoped that he would be able to find his way back to the road.

He shook off the gloom and worry, cursing himself as he did. He could certainly tell east from west and north from south. The sun would be his guide for now. And, later, if necessary, he could use the stars and moon to show him the correct way.

It got dark before he found the road, and he decided to stop. There was plenty of starlight to ride by, but both mules and Buffalo 2 needed to rest. It took almost no time to set up his cold camp, all the while wishing he had shot an antelope when he had the chance, or even some of the other game—he had seen plenty of turkeys and even some deer—he had come across during the day. He sighed. He had nothing to make a fire with anyway, and he was not much in favor of raw antelope, though like any other man of his background, he would eat whatever was at hand in starvin' times.

Irritated at himself, he ate a little jerky and then turned in, hoping that the land would not start roiling around him again as it had that morning. He could go the rest of his life without ever encountering such a thing again and be quite happy about it.

With no fire and no real camp to strike, he was ready to move on shortly after arising. Before going to sleep, he had checked the stars, made sure he had been going in the right direction, and then set himself a small stone marker for the morning.

After loading the pack mule and saddling Beelzebub, he climbed into the saddle and then checked his marker. With a nod, he pulled out, more confident in finding his way, though still unhappy about having to traverse such a wide-open land.

With relief, he hit the Camino Real late in the morning, and turned south. Several miles later he came across the camp White Bear and Ortega had used the night before. He stopped briefly to check sign and then to drink from the Rio Bravo nearby. He filled his gourd canteen and then hit the trail again, pushing a little harder in hopes of overtaking his two friends before dark.

That was not to be, however. He did, though, find a better camping spot than he had the night before—there was enough wood from the bushes and stunted trees to make a fire, and there was water close by. He tied the mules off and then moved toward some scrubby brush a little ways off. There he shot three prairie chickens and carried them back to camp. After unloading and unsaddling the mules and tending to them, he made a fire. While coffee heated, and the fire grew hotter, he plucked and gutted the prairie chickens. He hung two over the fire on sticks, and left the third sitting there for the time being.

Hungry, he didn't let the first chicken get fully done before he was gnawing away at it, tossing the bones into the brush, dripping grease and even a little blood all over himself. Not that he cared. Being a fastidious eater had never been one of his strong points.

The second prairie chicken was much more done and somewhat more tasty because of it. When he had polished that off—with a little help from Buffalo 2—he put the third bird over the fire to cook. Then he leaned back, lit his pipe and relaxed, with his pipe in one hand and a mug of coffee in the other.

He ate the third prairie chicken for his breakfast, again sharing some with the Newfoundland, though the dog had caught and eaten several pack mice that morning already.

Not wanting to waste any more time, Barlow hurriedly loaded the pack mule and saddled Beelzebub. Then he rode out, heading south at a good pace, planning to catch up to his friends before long. But they must've been setting a pretty good pace, too, Barlow thought as he rode, since the hours and miles slipped by and he did not see them. He decided to keep riding for a little while after dark. The road was well marked, and the starlight and moonlight allowed him to see enough to move along slowly.

He stopped now and again and looked around, hoping to spot something that might give him a clue to where White Bear and Ortega were. Finally, about two hours past full dark, he spotted a fire in the distance. Still, he moved cautiously. There was no certainty that it was his two friends out there. It could be anyone. But as he edged up, he could hear their voices, and knew it was them.

Not wanting to get shot by two nervous companions, he shouted, "Hey, boys, I'm comin' in!"

12

"TOOK YOU LONG enough to catch up to us, old chap," White Bear said with some sarcasm in his voice.

"Well, hoss," Barlow said as he climbed out of the saddle, "if I'd known you was gonna run like a scared rabbit till you was almost in Chihuahua, I would've made a little more haste. As it was, I figured you was gonna take your time once you got a few miles from that spot that spooked you so much. Not keep goin' like Ol' Scratch was on your tail."

"Who is this Old Scratch?" Ortega asked.

"Satan his own self, hoss," Barlow responded as he walked his horse and the pack mule to where the other animals were. "The way you boys must've been ridin', you must've thunk he was right behind you."

"We did not ride fast," Ortega protested. "You were too slow."

Barlow grinned a little. "Mayhap, hoss. Mayhap. But this goddamn mule was sure some skittish about bein' took back." He began unsaddling Beelzebub, while his two companions unloaded the supplies from the pack mule.

Done, the three sat at the fire, and Barlow hungrily tore into the antelope meat that cooked there, and downed some coffee. "You boys have any trouble on the trail since that damn earthquake?" he asked between bites.

"No, old chap," White Bear said. He still was a little nervous, worrying that his medicine might've gone bad and that this had brought on the earthquake. But he couldn't think of anything that he had done that might've caused his medicine to go bad.

"Glad to hear it. What next, Manuel?" Barlow asked.

"We head to the desert, though it will be some time before we get there, really. Couple of weeks, if we have no trouble. Then we head west."

Barlow nodded. "Well, it's robe time for this ol' critter. We got us a heap of travelin' to do, so I suggest you boys turn in, too." Without waiting to see if they did, Barlow got his sleeping robe and stretched it out. He shrugged off his heavy blanket coat, and slid into the sleeping robe. He was asleep within minutes of his head touching down.

The trail dropped a little with each passing day, though they were still in high desert. Two days after Barlow had caught up with his two companions, they rode into Socorro, which resembled Albuquerque, Santa Fe, and Taos—adobe houses, drab and small, the only highlights being the bright red chili ristras; a few who considered themselves still running things, strutting around in the tight-fitting pants with the conchos up the outer seam and the short jackets with braided gold thread; men, looking tough and uncompromising; the women, young and often beautiful, dressed in such a way as to excite a man's imagination, though without really revealing more than an an-

kle or shoulder when their serapes were off inside. The
centerpiece of the town was, as usual, the Catholic church
on the plaza. There were street vendors with their carts of
food and goods; cantinas that sent streams of delightful
aromas around the plaza.

The land was flat, for the most part, though mountains
could be seen in the distance. The temperatures were considerably warmer than they had been in Santa Fe and
Taos. All in all, it seemed a comfortable, inviting place.
The visitors did not draw too much attention, and Barlow
figured that the American presence after the war was not
felt much here yet.

The three men found a livery stable and left their animals there before heading out on foot for a cantina. They
stopped at the first one they came to and stepped inside.
It seemed a fine enough place. The inside was heavy with
tantalizing aromas, it did not appear to be overcrowded and
there were several women who looked at the new arrivals
with some interest. They took a table, and Buffalo 2 lay
down alongside Barlow's chair.

A fair-haired, fair-skinned young woman came up to
the table and started speaking Spanish. Barlow looked at
her in surprise, but waited until Ortega had translated—
she was asking what they wanted. They ordered through
Ortega, and the young woman bounced away, bright and
cheery.

"She ain't no Mexican, is she, hoss?" Barlow asked
Ortega.

"*Sí.*"

"But she don't look like no other Mexican woman I've
seen."

Ortega shrugged. "Light-skinned Mexicans exist,
amigo, but most are deep in the heart of Mexico, not out
here on the fringes. I don't know how she got here, but
here she is."

"She sure is a purty thing, hoss," Barlow said with a grin. "I think it might be time to put Nebuchadnezzar out to grass," he added with a laugh.

"What did he just say, *amigo*?" Ortega asked, looking at White Bear.

"The bloody bastard wants to engage in sexual intercourse with yon fair lady," White Bear said flatly.

"Don't you, *amigo*?" Ortega asked. "I do. With her or another *señorita* who looks as good. Or not as good. Or maybe even not so good at all."

The three burst into laughter.

When the woman returned with a jug of whiskey and three glasses, Barlow asked, "Do you speak English, *señorita*?"

"Very leetle," she replied with a dazzling smile.

"What's your name?"

"Teresita." She smiled wonderfully again. "And you, *señor*?"

"Will Barlow." He paused, then decided he would get nowhere with shyness and reserve. "Would you like to spend some time with me this evening?" he asked.

She looked confused, and without asking, Ortega translated for her. The smile came back more luminous than ever. *"Sí!"* she said with great enthusiasm.

Barlow's grin matched hers for intensity. "When can I see you? What time?"

Ortega translated and then said to Barlow, "Two hours, *amigo*. She will be free then."

"Two hours is a long time, *señorita*," Barlow said, looking at her, but knowing Ortega would translate.

Her eyes never left his face as she replied through Ortega, "Not too long, *señor*. Time to eat and rest a little."

Barlow nodded, and Teresita left once again.

"Two hours'll give you plenty of time to eat, as well as find someplace to take her, *amigo*," Ortega said.

"Aye, and time enough for you to find some companionship for me and our Mexican friend here, old chap," White Bear said flatly.

"You're on your own, hoss. I saw Teresita first and was the only one here who had the stones to say somethin'." He grinned widely, quite pleased with himself.

"Well, it's clear this *gringo* here won't help us, White Bear," Ortega said. "So we'll have to do what we can. *Perdon, por favor,*" he added, rising. "I will be right back."

White Bear and Barlow watched as Ortega approached a table at which several young women were sitting. He bent and began talking softly, using his most charming manner. A few minutes later, he strolled back to his own table, strutting like a peacock. He sat, grinning from ear to ear.

"Well?" Barlow asked impatiently. "What happened?"

"What do you think, *señor*?" Ortega countered. "Do you think I would fail in this matter?"

"Dammit, jist tell us what's goin' on, hoss."

"You see that lovely *señorita* with the red scarf?" When the two others nodded, he added, "I will be spending the evening with her."

"And what about ol' sourpuss White Bear there, hoss?" Barlow asked.

"Oh, him." He laughed. "He has the one with the blue blouse." He laughed again. "I told her you were a strange Englishman," he added, still laughing. "She doesn't know what an Englishman is, of course, but to her it sounds interesting and exciting. So see that you don't disappoint her, eh?"

"I'll do my best, old chap," White Bear said dryly.

Minutes later, Teresita arrived bearing platters of food. She placed them on the table and left, returning moments later with more food. The three men dug in, enjoying the various dishes—savory *pollo relleno*, a stuffed chicken;

corn-husk-wrapped tamales; tortillas; chili con carne; *caldo de cordero*, a sheep stew. All was washed down with goat's milk and whiskey, then coffee. Throughout the meal, Barlow offered pieces of just about everything to Buffalo 2, who enjoyed it all, and constantly wanted more.

Sated, the three leaned back and began puffing tobacco in one form or another.

Finally Barlow knocked the ashes from his pipe into one of the bowls on the table. "Well, boys, reckon we ought to find us someplace where we can git some robe time."

"I think the livery is out, old chap," White Bear said sarcastically.

Barlow grimaced at him. As they rose to leave, Teresita showed up again. "You go, *Señor* Barlow?" she asked, worry coating her grayish eyes.

Barlow nodded. "But only long enough to git a room to stay at," he said, letting Ortega translate. He was rewarded by a warm smile and a light touch on his fuzzy cheek, a touch that sent a thrill through him.

At the appointed time, Barlow was at the cantina, waiting eagerly for Teresita. Actually, he arrived a little early, and paced nervously outside for a while, wondering all the while whether Teresita had played him for a fool and had gone home to have a good laugh.

So it was with considerable relief that he spotted her walking toward the door. He pushed inside, smiling. She grinned back, and slid an arm through his. Together they walked out and up the street to the small adobe inn where he and the others had each taken a room.

As Barlow closed the door behind him, after letting Teresita in first, she turned and stepped up close to him. Taking his freshly shaven cheeks in her soft hands she kissed him lightly on the lips. Barlow wrapped his huge arms around her thin shoulders and pulled her close, deepening the kiss, his tongue playing tag with hers.

She finally pulled back, smiling softly at him. He returned it. Then he removed his belt and weapons and tossed them to the floor away from the bed.

Buffalo 2 looked at him, as if he couldn't believe his master was going to go through this strange ritual with another woman. With a grunt, he lay along one wall, big head on his front paws. Then he ignored the humans.

Barlow turned and blew out one of the two candles. When he turned back, Teresita was standing there naked, her skirt, blouse and serape puddled around her empty shoes. Her arms hung by her sides, neither advertising nor hiding her body.

"*¡Muy bueno!*" Barlow said with a huge smile. He was pleased with what he saw—a small but well-rounded body, skin almost as white as his own, ample breasts, though not overly so, the nipples poking out strongly, mostly from the cold, a nice flare to her hips, the patch of soft hair covering her womanhood lighter than any he had ever seen before, a downy blond shade, well-formed legs. "*¡Muy bueno!*" he said again.

"Cold," she said, hugging herself. She turned to pull the covers down on the bed, offering Barlow a fine view of her supple back and perfectly rounded posterior.

As Teresita climbed into the fairly solid-looking bed, Barlow hastily shucked his garments and threw them aside. Teresita smiled widely, quite pleased with what she saw, too—a man broader than any she had ever seen, with a bull-like neck, immense shoulders, slabs of muscle across his scarred chest, and manly parts that held great promise.

He slipped under the covers with her, sliding an arm under her head. He kissed her, softly, then harder. She replied in kind.

His hand slid down her sleek body, running up and down her side, as well as the side of her thigh, sometimes straying to her buttocks. She laid her leg over his, and ran her foot up and down it. He didn't quite know how she managed to do it, but suddenly her toes were tickling his manhood and associated parts. He had already been growing but now his lance truly sprang up, ready to get into the action.

Barlow's hand began kneading Teresita's breast, squeezing, releasing, pinching the nipple lightly. Teresita sighed with pleasure, and fell more onto her back, opening herself up to him. Barlow began kissing a path from her lips to her toes, lingering here and there at the more interesting sites she presented. He threw back the blankets, the cold bothering neither one of them now in the heat of their passion.

Kneeling between her legs, Barlow lifted her buttocks in his powerful hands, bringing her flower to his lips. He could not resist, since she was so light-haired there. He just had to get close to it, savor it. And he did, much to Teresita's vocal delight. Several times. He grinned as he watched her breasts and the skin above them, all the way to her neck, redden with the flush of pleasure searing through her.

Finally he placed her back down, and Teresita spread her legs wider, inviting him to paradise. A little worried about his great size and her small frame, he gingerly eased up and entered her, sending thrills bouncing around inside his body.

"Come close," she whispered.

"I might be too heavy," he responded, not sure she understood.

But she apparently did. "No. Is *bueno.*"

He nodded, and scrunched up closer to her, sliding his full length into her. Still concerned a little about the mass of his body, he propped himself on knees and hands, as he gazed into her bright eyes for a few moments, before he both kissed her and began moving his hips up and down.

Teresita threw her legs around the small of his back and held on strongly, kissing back as hard as she received, letting him set the pace. She wrapped her arms around his neck and held his lips on her, and he increased speed and intensity in his movements.

With her legs locked around his back, she lifted her buttocks up off the bed, and she arched her back and ground her groin against his as hard as she could, all the while screaming her joy into his mouth.

Moments later, his neck pulled free from her arms, and he huffed and puffed while reaching a climax that was every bit as powerful as hers had been.

They collapsed on the bed, front to front, breathing heavily, smiling at each other.

"*¡Muy bueno!*" they said at the same time, and laughed.

13

TERESITA WAS AS hungry for him in the morning as he was for her. He awoke with her gently stroking his shaft. He smiled at her and pulled her up to where he could kiss her good and properly.

When they had finished and rested a little, they slowly got dressed. Without him having to say anything, Teresita knew he would be leaving soon. She wished he would stay for a while, but she sensed he was on some kind of important business. So she said nothing about it, but she couldn't help hoping this massive battering ram of a man would come by this way again and visit her.

Barlow and Teresita met White Bear, Ortega and their two women in the cantina, and ate heartily of some egg and chili dish with tortillas on the side. They tried hot chocolate, which Barlow and White Bear had never had before, despite their time in Santa Fe and Taos. They had been offered it, but they had thought it foolish and strange. But somehow, it seemed the right thing to have with this morning's repast.

While the hot chocolate was quite tasty, all three men

had to finish off the meal with coffee. White Bear had asked for tea, since he had had none in so long a time, but the cantina didn't have any. White Bear wasn't even sure they knew what he was talking about.

With lovemaking and breakfast over, Barlow swiftly, almost automatically shifted his focus from the woman to the job at hand. He didn't mean to be gruff with Teresita, but he was a little, finally telling his two companions that it was time to go.

With long, final kisses lingering on their lips, the three men headed for the livery stable, loaded the supplies, saddled their horses and rode out of Socorro, not bothering to look back.

Over the next several days, the scenery and landscape changed again, much like it had between Santa Fe and Albuquerque. There was far more cactus, and of a much wider variety; stunted, gnarly mesquite trees became more and more common, even though cottonwoods still grew along the river and the few streams they passed; and there were creosote bushes, with their waxy-looking leaves.

They saw an increasing number of rattlesnakes, too. These were big, much larger than Barlow and White Bear were used to. They hunted antelope and deer as they rode for each evening's meal, and they spotted bobcat and possum in abundance. Neither Barlow nor White Bear wanted to eat either critter, though both considered killing a bobcat and making a hat out of the animal's fur. But they decided that could wait.

One day while riding slowly along, three abreast, as they usually did when possible, a critter skittered across the road in front of them and into the bushes.

"What the hell was that?" Barlow asked.

"Armadillo, I think," White Bear replied. "There are many here. Would you like one to eat?"

"I don't think so, hoss," Barlow said cautiously. "I

didn't git much of a look at that critter, but from what I saw, he didn't look like he'd make tasty feedin' at all."

"I will show you what they look like," Ortega said, and trotted off the side of the road where the armadillo had disappeared. A moment later there was a gunshot and soon after, Ortega came riding back holding a fairly large creature by the tail. "Here," he said, holding it out, "this is an armadillo."

"That's the ugliest goddamn critter I've ever laid lights on, hoss," Barlow said in disgust.

"I'd have to agree with you, old chap," White Bear said. "Bloody hideous thing it is."

"You mean to tell me that your people eat them goddamn things?" Barlow asked, still repulsed by the animal.

"No, not my people," Ortega said hastily. "But some of the Indians out in these parts do."

Barlow spit into the dirt. "Git rid of it, hoss," he ordered. "Before this mornin's feedin' comes shootin' back up and out of me."

Ortega laughed uproariously, but flung the thing away. Buffalo 2 trotted over and sniffed at the armadillo. He looked uncertain, and tore away a small piece. He quickly dropped it and ran off, shaking his head, while the men laughed.

Two days later, as they were riding along early one afternoon, they pulled to a halt when they heard a strange noise. For a few dreadful seconds, they thought it might be the beginnings of another earthquake, but they soon realized it was not like that sound at all.

"What is it, hoss?" Barlow asked.

"Javelina," Ortega said, trying to pick out just where the sound was coming from.

"What the hell's a javelina?"

"It is a piglike animal," Ortega explained. "But it has

tusks, making it ugly and very fierce. I think we should hunt some."

"Not if it's anything like that bloody armadillo," White Bear said quickly.

"No, *señores*," Ortega said. "It tastes like *el puerco*— pig. You have had pork, *señores*, yes?"

Both nodded.

"This is a little tougher, but has the same flavor. Mixed with a few chilies, it would be good eating. And something different."

Barlow and White Bear looked at each other and then nodded.

Ortega led them off the trail toward a small, barren mountain, but stopped well before they got there. "In there, *amigos*," Ortega said, pointing to a patch of harsh, thorny scrub brush. "I will go around and try to flush them out. When they come, you shoot." He rode off.

A few minutes later, Barlow and White Bear heard Ortega shouting from beyond the briar patch. In seconds, several tusked pigs came charging out of the thicket, looking ready to kill anything that got in their way, and apparently having the armament to do it.

Though startled, Barlow brought his rifle up quickly and dropped one of the running animals. White Bear got another one with an arrow just afterward. They sat there and waited until the javelinas were gone, and Ortega had returned.

The Mexican got off his horse and looked down at one dead javelina and then the other. *"Bueno,"* he said with a grin. "Come, we'll butcher them here. I don't want to carry these things with us. Too big and heavy."

Following Ortega's lead, the American and the Shoshoni carefully carved out some meat.

That night, Ortega put a bunch of the meat into a pot with various chili peppers and spices they had brought along from Albuquerque and let the concoction simmer for some time. Then, as a surprise, he pulled out a piece of cheesecloth that was inside a piece of folded leather tied tight. Inside were half a dozen corn tortillas the Mexican had brought from Socorro. He scooped some of the stew into bowls for his two companions, then gave them each a tortilla. He got some for himself and sat. "Eat up, *amigos,*" he said with a grin. He spooned some into his mouth after blowing on it a bit to cool it.

"What the hell," Barlow said. He got a spoonful, blew on it, and slipped it into his mouth. It was hot, but tasty. He took a small bite of the tortilla, and the flavors blended together perfectly. "Goddamn, hoss," he said, "this here's right tasty."

"Told you, *amigo,*" Ortega said with a proud grin.

White Bear had to agree, and the three polished off nearly the whole pot of stew and easily all the tortillas. "Well, it ain't buffler," Barlow said as he stretched out on his back to give his stomach some breathing room, "but it's damn close to as good."

"I believe you're right, old chap," White Bear said.

They fell asleep where they were, too full and sated to want to move. While it was still cold out at night, it wasn't too bad, and they just pulled their coats over them while sleeping. That and being close to the fire was enough.

They ate more javelina in the morning, this time just roasted over the flames. It wasn't as good, but that was because they had no tortillas left, they all thought.

Soon they were on the road again, moseying along, trying to spare the animals. As they rode, Barlow said, "You know, Manuel, if I'd known this road was gonna be this good and this well-marked, I might've headed out here on my own."

"*Sí,* the road is good here, *amigo,*" Ortega replied seriously. "But in due time we will turn west, where there is no road at all. Then you would be in trouble without me."

"We would've been in trouble without you already, old chap," White Bear said seriously.

"Muchas gracias."

The days soon grew tiresome, boring, monotonous. With the exception of hunting, there was little to do, and less to see. The land was flat in most places, though small, jagged mountains rose up here and there. They were mostly barren and offered little in the way of something interesting to look at.

The dullness of the journey once more gave Barlow too much time to think, and he could not stop his thoughts from turning to Anna. He wondered where she was, how she was being treated, how she had been treated all along, whether she was with good people or bad, though he decided that no people who had her could be good. He worried about whether she would know him—or whether he would know her. She had grown considerably, he guessed, in the five years she had been gone, and he often had the chilling thought that not only would she not know him, she would want nothing to do with him.

Despite his concerns and worries, his senses continued to check the world around him. It had become an automatic thing by now, and he didn't even notice that he noted the movement of brush against the wind, the unusual flight of a bird, anything that might be out of place. That and Buffalo 2's heightened senses had kept the two of them alive for a good long time.

So it was with some concern that he noticed that Buffalo 2 was acting strangely, as if he knew something or someone was around but couldn't place it or figure out what it was. Barlow had sort of the same feeling, as if someone was watching them travel, but not so close as to be seen or even heard. The country had become rougher, with more of the small, harsh-looking mountains around, sometimes within shouting distance of the road. Barlow figured that an army could be hiding out here and he wouldn't know about it. That feeling did not sit well with him.

He felt compelled to mention it, and at the fire that night, he said, "I been gittin' the feelin' we're bein' watched, boys." It was said with irritation in his voice.

"I've been feeling the same, old chap," White Bear added. "Didn't want to say anything lest someone think I was bloody barmy."

"Barmy?" Ortega asked.

"*Loco.*"

"Ah, I see," Ortega noted.

"Even Buffler seems to know somethin' ain't right," Barlow said. "It's like there's ghosts about or something." The thought was ridiculous, but it was there nonetheless. Suddenly he looked at Ortega. "You've been mighty quiet over there, hoss," he said a bit harshly. "You know anything about any of this?"

"No, *señor*," Ortega said not very convincingly.

"You got some *amigos* out there plannin' to raise hair on some damn *americano* and his Shoshoni *amigo*?" Barlow demanded.

"Of course not, *señor*," Ortega said indignantly.

"Then what the hell's goin' on, hoss?"

"We are in Apache country," Ortega said quietly.

"Why didn't you bloody say something before now, old chap?" White Bear asked, annoyed.

"I was hoping we could get through here without trouble. I didn't want to alarm you."

"Goddamn, hoss," Barlow spat, "leavin' us in the dark on this makes it worse. If we knew we was goin' into Apache country, we could've been more on the lookout." His irritation was growing.

"Do you think the bloody Apaches are watching us, old chap?"

Ortega shrugged. "Could be. They're demons, those Indians. Move around this country like ghosts, popping up where they're least expected, causin' trouble and disappearing."

"They as nasty as I've heard?" Barlow asked.

Ortega nodded. "Nastiest Indians you'll ever meet," he noted.

"Worse than the Blackfoot?" Barlow asked, surprised.

"Much worse, *amigo*. They know every inch of their land intimately. As I said, they flit around through here like ghosts, appearing and disappearing at will. They have stamina you couldn't believe, and usually travel twice as far and twice as fast on foot as men on horseback. And unlike the Blackfeet or any of those other Indians up north, the Apaches never quit. They don't take a few losses and pull back, thinking their medicine has gone bad." He shrugged and looked at White Bear, adding, "Sorry, *amigo*."

White Bear nodded. He could understand the man's disbelief in such a system. He sometimes questioned it himself, when his Anglo upbringing came to the fore, as it was wont to do now and again.

"Do they git along with Mexicans, hoss? Or Americans?" Barlow asked, still annoyed.

"They don't like the Mexicans at all, *amigo*," Ortega said flatly. "For many, many years, my people and the Apaches have made war on each other. It has often been brutal, with unforgivable sins on both sides. But if the Apaches would only leave us alone, not attack our *ranchos* and other places, there wouldn't be so much trouble."

"Your people invaded their homeland, hoss," Barlow said. "I can understand how they'd be unhappy with sich doin's. Still," he added with a sigh, "you'd think that after all these years of blood and death they might figure out how to git along together, though I reckon it ain't no different from anywhere else."

"Is there anything we can do, old chap?" White Bear asked. "About the bloody Apaches, I mean."

Ortega shook his head. "Just be more alert than usual, and be prepared for a surprise attack sometime."

"You're scared to death of them boys, ain't you, hoss?" Barlow asked with sudden realization. "You didn't tell us before now because you was afraid to even mention them critters." His eyes were accusatory.

"*Sí, señor,*" Ortega said quietly. "I am ashamed of it."

"No need to be ashamed, hoss. All of us has been afraid of somethin' or someone. If these Apaches're as tough and mean as you say, it jist makes sense to be afraid of 'em. Jist as long as you can do your part, if them critters attack."

"I will, *amigo,*" Ortega vowed.

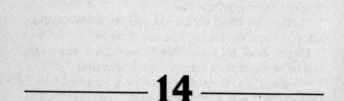

14

THE SMALL GROUP rode on, tense, wary, senses heightened in an attempt to find out where the Apaches were out there. But it was all in vain. The Indians remained hidden by the brush, the rocks, hills, mountains, even the air itself, it seemed to the travelers.

It was annoying, and worse, stressful for all. More than once Barlow and Buffalo 2 veered off the trail in a search for sign, but he could find nothing. It was spooky to him. Never before had he been around Indians who left no sign that they were there. But these Apaches—if, indeed, that's what they were—seemed to be able to pass through this land invisibly, making no mark on the land.

It wore on the nerves of all three men. Even Buffalo 2 seemed to be bothered by the increased tensions. Another two days went by, and while he still had the feeling that they were being watched, Barlow began to think that he—and the others—had conjured up the danger. That it was not really there. Nobody could follow them closely, especially in those areas where the land was flat and open, without being seen, or at the least leaving some marks of their passage.

"You think there's really Injins out there, hoss?" Barlow asked Ortega over the evening fire—a poor thing it was, too—two nights later.

"*Sí,*" the Mexican replied. "They are there all right, *señor.*"

"Then what the hell're they waitin' for?" Barlow asked. "Why'n't they jist attack us?"

"Who knows the mind of any Indi . . ." Ortega glanced at White Bear, ". . . almost any Indian?" he corrected himself. "The Apaches in particular are hard to understand, from everything I've heard about them. They are like the wind—here one moment, gone the next."

"I think you're jist too taken with ghosty stories and sich, hoss," Barlow said flatly. "Any Injins I've ever run into would've attacked by now."

"But the Apaches aren't just any Indians, *señor,*" Ortega insisted. "They are demons, I tell you again, *amigo.* And do devilish things." He made the sign of the cross hurriedly, unashamed that he was doing so in front of the others. "I think they are following us just to toy with us, *amigos.* They will stay out of our sight and hearing for as long as they think it takes for us to become so filled with anxiety that we are not ourselves. Then, when our guard is down, they will attack."

"You been sneakin' some awardenty, hoss?" Barlow asked. "Maybe addled your brains in the doin'?"

"No, *señor,*" Ortega replied firmly. "You don't know the Apaches. You are used to Indians like the Blackfoot and Utes, and even the Shoshonis, like White Bear here. The Apaches are a *muy* different people. Don't ever doubt that, *señores.*"

"Well, I don't think there're any of those critters out

there, hoss," Barlow said with certainty in his voice. "I think you're jist spooked, mayhap still from that earthquake."

"I do not lie about this, *señor*," Ortega snapped. "Those devils are out there, and they will attack us, when they think the time is right for it, and not one moment before."

"What do you think, White Bear?" Barlow asked.

The Indian sat in silence for a bit, trying to figure it out. Despite his American-English upbringing, he was still a Shoshoni at heart, and often in thought. He believed in the spirits, both good and bad. And, if whatever Ortega was saying about the Apaches were true, they were definitely bad spirits, and that was something he did not want to deal with.

Finally he shrugged. "I tend to believe Manuel. At least some bloody what. He's familiar with this country—and its inhabitants, old chap. We are not. I think maybe you've gotten too cocky, my friend."

"Mayhap," Barlow responded. "But I don't think so. I jist figured we've all been spooked by some of the doin's that've gone on whilst we've been on the trail, and we're letting our minds git carried away with visions and sounds that ain't really there."

"I hope you're right, old chap," White Bear said uncomfortably.

The stress from nervously awaiting an attack at any moment continued to build over the next couple of days, until all three men—and the dog—were edgy, uneasy. They growled at each other over the smallest things, argued more than they ever had and more than once almost came to blows.

Barlow went to bed the next night, angry at himself, and angry at his two companions. He still felt that they were being watched, and he did not like the feeling. Yet he was still trying to convince himself that there was no one out there, and not doing a very good job, but his two friends were worse than he in their beliefs about the supernatural powers of the Apaches.

His slumber, as it had been for the past several nights, was uneasy, restless. And when Buffalo 2 awoke him with a hushed growl just about the time dawn was breaking, he was grumpy about it. "Hush up that noise, Buffler," he commanded.

But the dog continued to snarl. Barlow glanced at the dog. From the Newfoundland's bared fangs and raised hackles, Barlow realized there was something to Buffalo 2's warning. He snapped to alertness. He started to slide out of his sleeping robe, pulling his rifle with him. At the same time, he hissed, "White Bear! Manuel! Wake up, boys!"

Like Barlow, the Shoshoni came awake grouchy, but his senses were on full alert within a second or two, as soon as he realized from Barlow's voice that something was amiss. He slipped out of his sleeping robes and quickly strung his bow.

Ortega awoke testy, and struggled to shed the annoyance of being shaken out of his sleep like this. He was about to say something about it when an arrow thudded into his blankets, barely missing his chest. *"¡Madre de dios!"* he said quietly. He grabbed his rifle and scuttled away from the blanket bed as another arrow embedded itself in the ground where he had been lying only moments before.

There was little cover there—just some small, scraggly bushes and a few rocks. Barlow managed to slither over and behind one of the latter. It provided little protection, but it was better than being completely exposed as he had been.

He swore silently when he couldn't see any enemies. It was as if they blended into the land itself. But he knew they were out there—unless arrows were falling from the sky, which he knew could not be true. He looked over his shoulder, checking the area behind him. He saw no one there either, but that didn't mean some Apaches weren't there, as hidden behind him as they were in front of him.

He lay there sweating, wondering if the Apaches would ever show themselves. He was worried about moving from the spot, unsure whether the enemies were still out there waiting for a better target, or if they had slipped away.

White Bear was scrunched up behind a bush twenty feet to Barlow's right, and Ortega, between the two, was trying to hide behind a rock that was far smaller than Barlow's. He looked considerably frightened.

"These critters got any hankerin' for mule flesh, hoss?" Barlow asked quietly, glancing over at Ortega.

"Sometimes I think they like mules more than horses, *señor*."

"Damn," Barlow muttered. "White Bear," he shouted, "we best make sure they ain't aimin' to steal our animals."

The Shoshoni just nodded. He got down on his belly, slung his bow across his back and started slithering on his stomach toward the small herd of horses and mules.

Barlow began doing the same thing, rifle cradled across his forearms. He was farther away, and rushed to catch up to White Bear.

Suddenly the Shoshoni jumped to his feet, somehow having his bow and several arrows in hand as he did. He quickly fired off three missiles at nothing, or so it seemed to Barlow. But he heard someone falling over near the herd. Then he spotted a shadowy figure that seemed to come right out from the ground just to White Bear's right. The Shoshoni would not have enough time to shoot the enemy with an arrow, nor drop his bow and draw his war club.

Barlow pushed up onto one knee, brought his rifle up and fired, hardly taking aim. Because of it, he only winged the Apache, who disappeared behind some brush.

Two more Apaches popped up out of nowhere, it seemed, and charged forward, war clubs in hand. One headed for White Bear and the other for Barlow. It was the first time Barlow had gotten a look at an Apache, and he was not very impressed. The man charging him was quite short, and thin, though wiry. His dark, mean-looking face had a few stripes of white paint on it, a thin slit of a mouth, and dark, glittering eyes that seemed to hold little evidence of humanity. His rather short, black hair was held down by a cloth headband. He wore a Mexican peon cloth shirt, a long breechcloth of the same material, and moccasins that were up to his thighs, protecting his legs from brambles and such.

Barlow took all that in with a couple of seconds as the Apache roared at him. Then he shifted his rifle and grabbed it in both hands near the muzzle, then swung it.

The Apache somehow managed to duck under it without slowing his speed, and then plowed into Barlow, driving him back. Barlow's heel hit a stone, and he fell heavily on his back, an involuntary grunt rushing up his windpipe and out. The Apache landed mostly on top of him, and swiftly shifted to where he was straddling Barlow's stomach, his war club raised.

"Not so goddamn fast, hoss," Barlow muttered as his left hand snaked up to grab the Apache's wrist, stopping the war club from descending.

The warrior used his left hand to punch Barlow in the face twice, before the American managed to grab the Indian's other wrist. He held the Apache's hands away from him, stretched out to the sides. They seemed to be at an impasse, neither able to do much without also giving the other an advantage of some kind.

Then Buffalo 2 came running over, snarling, teeth bared. The dog grabbed the Indian's shirt at the back, and a piece of flesh with it and used all his massive strength to tug the warrior backward.

Between that and Barlow's mighty strength pushing from the front, the Apache had little chance. He suddenly jerked his wrists free from Barlow's grasp and fell to the side. His shirt ripped, leaving Buffalo 2 with a hunk of cloth in his mouth, and the Apache ran off, his mostly bare back bleeding.

Barlow quickly pushed himself up and yanked out a pistol, figuring to finish the warrior off. He fired hastily, missing the fleeing Apache. "Dammit all," he muttered. He glanced around, looking for more attacks, but it seemed the only Apache left in the immediate vicinity was the one grappling with White Bear.

"Buffler," Barlow said sharply, "go help White Bear. Go on."

The dog raced over toward the two struggling figures. He stopped short and bit a piece out of the back of the Apache's thigh.

The warrior did not shout or scream, but that leg buckled on him. With White Bear's added impetus, he fell to the side. White Bear swiftly knelt and slid his knife blade into the Apache's chest. In moments, the foe had died.

White Bear reached out and yanked off the Apache's headband, then grabbed a shank of his hair, ready to take the scalp.

"Don't, White Bear!" Barlow shouted, trotting up. When White Bear looked up at him, Barlow said, "Don't raise his hair, hoss."

"Why not, dammit?" White Bear growled. "I counted coup on this bloody bastard, and it's my right to take his scalp."

"I know it's your right, hoss," Barlow said evenly. "But it ain't the wise thing to do right now."

"What do you mean, old chap?" White Bear asked, some of his English-trained sensibilities returning.

"I don't know if it'll work with the damn Apaches, but sich a thing has worked before. We don't scalp him or cut him or anything. We leave 'em here nice and whole. Mayhap those Apaches will think we've done a good thing and leave us the hell alone."

White Bear rose, sliding the knife into the sheath. "It's worth a try, old chap," he said, back to his usual self.

The two, now joined by Ortega, went to check on the horses. As they did, Buffalo 2 discovered the body of another Apache, two arrows in his chest. Barlow lifted the bloody body and carried it to where the other one lay, and gently set it down next to the other. He straightened both corpses, then went back to help with the horses.

The three travelers stoked up the fire and broke their fast sitting only a few feet from the bodies, which they ignored except to toss rocks at some coyotes who had the scent of blood in their nostrils.

"You know, old chap," White Bear said while eating, "if we just leave those bodies there, the coyotes'll get them as soon as we're out of sight. Which would ruin whatever good we were trying to create by leaving them whole."

"Reckon you're right, hoss," Barlow agreed. "You got any suggestions as to what we should do with 'em?"

"You remember those big boulders we passed maybe a quarter mile back?"

"Yep. Big round ones. Why?"

"We could put these fellows on top of one of those rocks. They'd be safe from the coyotes then."

"But not from the buzzards and sich scavenger birds."

"I don't think that the fellows who've been following

us and who attacked us this morning have gone far. I think they're still close by. They'll probably collect the bodies before we get back here after leaving them off."

Barlow nodded. It was the best they could do.

They finished eating, and then loaded the two bodies onto one of the pack mules and rode back to the site where they had spotted the rocks. It took considerable effort, but they finally got the corpses on the boulders and rode back to their camp. Ortega had the two other pack mules loaded and had only a little left over to put on the mule Barlow and White Bear had just used. They quickly loaded that animal and set off on their journey again.

The feeling that they were being watched still rode with them, hanging over them like a long serape. They continued being extra wary, but they were spooked now. They now knew for certain that the Apaches were out there watching them, but they still could not hear them or see them.

15

THE TENSION SURROUNDING the three men and the dog deepened until it was almost palpable. It was even worse than before, since they now knew for sure that they were under the watchful eyes of the Apaches. And there was nothing they could do about it. That was the most galling thing to all of them.

"I wish those heathen sons a bitches would jist come on out and fight us," Barlow grumbled the night after the attack. "Then we'd jist be done with it."

"This is the way they do things, *amigo*," Ortega said quietly, trying to quell some of his anxiety. "They drive a man to the breaking point like this, and then swoop down on him."

"Well, I ain't about to put up with such goddamn doin's for much longer, hoss, I can tell you that right away."

"Me either, old chaps," White Bear agreed.

"And just what will you do, *señores*?" Ortega asked.

"I ain't rightly sure," Barlow said, "but I'll damn certain figure somethin' out when the right time comes along."

The next day was even more nerve-wracking than the previous few, and the one after that was far worse. The uneasiness among the men was so thick, that Barlow wondered if they would have to cut their way through it.

They were silent at the night's meal, each knowing that to open his mouth on anything would be to invite trouble from his two companions. They were nervous, though not really scared. They figured they could account well for themselves once the battle was joined. But their nerves were on edge because of the dreaded anticipation, the wondering when the Apaches would attack for real.

Barlow climbed into his sleeping robes and lay there, hands laced behind his head, looking up at the night sky with its dazzling display of stars and wondering what—if anything—he could do to get the Apaches away from them. He supposed he could ride out and make a more diligent search for them, but he had begun to think that Ortega was right—that the Apaches were more like ghosts or spirits who could disappear and reappear at will.

Besides, a man out there alone, surrounded by Apaches, would be easy pickings for warriors as experienced and deadly as the Apaches were showing themselves to be. And if he went under then, what would become of Anna? No, he told himself firmly in his mind, it could not be risked.

He fell into an unsettled sleep with no solution in mind. He awoke the same way, knowing he should do something, wanting to do something, but unable to come up with a decent answer as to what. He sat at the fire and poured himself some coffee. At least they had that much. It did little to make the journey more bearable, really, but without it things would have been far worse.

A squabble broke out between White Bear and Ortega over near the horses and mules, and the two began to wrestle and punch each other.

"Goddamn," Barlow muttered. He set his coffee mug down and stomped over to the two combatants. He grabbed ahold of each one's shirt in a big paw and jerked them apart.

"This ain't no way for friends to act, boys," he said sternly, irritation creeping into his voice.

"It was all that bloody chap's fault," White Bear snapped. "Damn bean-eating, barmy bloody bastard."

"You red-skinned heathen devil," Ortega countered.

"What the hell is all this about?" Barlow demanded. "What set you two off agin each other?"

"That bloody chap over there insisted on having the last piece of meat on the fire."

"I started the fire, put the coffee on and had cooked that meat, damn you," Ortega snarled. "I figure I deserved that piece."

"You two morons were fightin' over a goddamn piece of meat?" Barlow roared. "Have you both lost all your reason? Goddamn fools." Barlow shoved them away to opposite sides. "We got half a goddamn javelina over there jist ready for roastin'. Now git on over there, the two of you, and put some meat on to cookin'. Enough meat for all of us. And stop this childish fightin'. We're supposed to be *amigos* here."

Barlow turned to head back to the fire, and Ortega jumped on his back, hands scrabbling for some kind of hold on the big man. Barlow fairly easily pried the Mexican's hands off his neck and twisted one of them until Ortega fell off his back and onto the ground with a hard thump.

Barlow knelt and grabbed Ortega's shirt. "Don't you ever come agin me another time, hoss," he growled. "Next time you do so, it'll be the last attack you make on anybody."

The Mexican nodded, his eyes frightened. He had suddenly realized just how close to death he had come, and how close to being pummeled into mush. He wanted to face neither of those things.

"I'm sorry, *señor*," Ortega said quietly. "I don't know what got into me."

Barlow nodded. Ortega seemed serious enough to him about it all. He could forgive, but he would not forget for a while. He would keep a close eye on Ortega for some time, just to make sure that the anxiety sparked by the Apaches hadn't made him go mad over the past several days.

They all sat at the fire, White Bear and Ortega glowering at each other, and Barlow ignoring them both. Buffalo 2 paid no attention either, gnawing as he was on a javelina bone.

As Barlow leaned back with a last cup of coffee and a pipeful of tobacco, his two friends started sniping at each other again. Barlow didn't really know what it was about, nor did he care. He just wanted the bickering to stop. On the other hand, he felt like joining in. They were all nervous, irritable and short of temper these days. *If only those damn Apaches hadn't come along,* he thought, *we would've been all right*. He was purely sick and tired of it all, disgusted with what it was doing to him and his friends, angry that he was so impotent against this unseen enemy, concerned with the possibility of an attack coming at any time. It was unnerving, and infuriating, and he had had enough of it.

Without really thinking about it, Barlow pushed to his feet. He left his rifle laying against a rock. To his friends' surprise, he pulled out his two single-shot pistols, as well as the Colt Paterson, and dropped them all to the ground. He spun on his heel and moved a few yards away from the fire. He stood for a moment, looking around, trying to spot the invisible Apaches. He could see none, as usual.

"What are you doing, *señor*?" a startled Ortega asked.

"Tryin' to put an end to this nonsense so we can git on with the task we've set," Barlow said flatly.

"Are you going to challenge them, old chap?" White Bear asked with a sneer. "Perhaps take on the whole Apache Nation?"

Barlow glared at him. He took a deep breath and in English bellowed, "Apaches, if you're out there, show yourselves, you chicken-hearted sacks of shit! C'mon out and fight me. Or parley. The choice is yours." He shut up and waited for an answer.

"The bloody damn fool is challenging them," White Bear said in wonder, and annoyance. "He's going to get us all killed."

"Maybe not, *amigo*," Ortega said. "The Apaches admire courage above all else. If they think he is serious, they'll come out and talk."

"I hope you're right."

Not having gotten a response, Barlow bellowed out his challenge again, adding, "What are you boys afeared of, eh? Us three ol' boys and one ol' dog? I had heard the Apaches were brave, courageous, tough. Warriors with no equal anywhere. Are they lies? Are you really a bunch of faint-hearted ol' women, wearin' skirts?"

Again he waited, but still there was nothing. Barlow turned his head. "C'mon over here, hoss," he said to Ortega. "Leave your guns there."

A frightened Manuel Ortega dropped his guns in the dirt and tentatively sidled up to Barlow.

"Tell 'em what I jist said, hoss. Word for word. Don't make no changes, don't try'n gussy it up. I want them stinkin' critters to know that I ain't scared of 'em." When he saw Ortega's hesitation, he ordered, "Tell 'em, hoss. Good and loud."

"I can't remember all you said, *señor*," Ortega said,

hoping this would get him out of having to do such an onerous and dangerous task.

"Then you translate it as I say it to you, hoss," Barlow said flatly. He started, offering the same basic challenge, embellishing it with a few more insults that he had before.

They waited in the silence, as the wind blew around them, ruffling their hair, the fringes on Barlow's pants, the short open front of Ortega's jacket.

A voice suddenly came out of nowhere, startling them, even though they had been hoping for it. "Tell your other man to put down his weapons," the disembodied voice said in Spanish.

Ortega translated for White Bear, who looked at Barlow. The former mountain man nodded slightly.

White Bear shrugged and lay down his bow and quiver of arrows. He also put down his only pistol. Then he marched over, head high, shoulders back, to stand next to Barlow and Ortega. He would not let these Apaches see any fear in him. He had faced tough warriors before, he could do it with these.

"We done what you asked," Barlow said, letting Ortega translate it into Spanish. "Now c'mon out. Unless you're afraid."

There were some moments of silence, then Apaches began to appear, almost as if they had been spit out by the earth itself, until there were a dozen of them.

"Come," Barlow said, "we will sit at my fire, we'll share food and coffee, and we'll parley. We mean you no harm, and we don't want to be harmed by you. There ain't no call for us to go fightin' each other. We got us enough enemies without makin' any more when it ain't necessary."

The Apaches looked doubtful.

"Good Lord Almighty," Barlow snapped, "you've been follerin' us for days now, you know we cain't have hid any surprises for you. You're the ones got all the odds in your favor. We're unarmed, you still have your weapons. Plus, as far as I know there could be a hundred more of your boys out there jist waitin' to raise our hair."

When Ortega finished translating all that, one of the Apaches nodded. "I am El Gato, as the Mexicans call me."

"The Cat?" Barlow asked Ortega just to make sure.

The Mexican nodded, saying, "I think they mean a big cat, like a puma."

Barlow said, "I am Will Barlow. The translator is Manuel Ortega, and the other of us is White Bear. He is a Shoshoni, from a tribe far, far to the north."

"We have heard of these Shoshonis," El Gato said. His face hardened even more than it had been. "They are brothers of our enemies, the Comanches."

"Sorry, old chap," White Bear said evenly, "but I've never met any bloody Comanches that I can recall."

El Gato looked at him in surprise. While he didn't know what White Bear had said, he knew it was in English. After Ortega translated that, El Gato nodded. He pointed to Buffalo 2.

"This here's Buffler," Barlow said, petting the animal's big head. "He's a special dog, one with many powers given by the spirits." He figured it wouldn't hurt to put a bit of fear into the Apaches.

"We sit," the Apache said in English.

They gathered around the pitifully small fire. Coffee was passed around, and then more put on the fire. Meat was divided so that all got at least some. When they were settled in, almost relaxed in each other's presence, Barlow could see no reason to dally, so he asked, "Why have you been follerin' us? And why'd you attack us the other day?"

"We do not like interlopers in our land," El Gato said

through Ortega. "Too many have come into the land of my people. It is time they stayed out."

"We ain't aimin' to stay here, hoss," Barlow replied. "We're jist passin' through."

"Many people have said that. And many have remained here, hunting our animals, using our water, killing my people."

"We ain't aimin' to kill none of your people. We had to do so the other day jist to protect ourselves, but if you had left us alone, we'd never had kilt none of your people." He paused, then added, "And we did not scalp or otherwise mutilate your warriors. We put them where the scavengers could not get to them. You found them?"

El Gato nodded.

"We did that so you would know our purpose here is not to cause trouble with the Apaches. We want no fight with you or your people. All we ask is what you ask—to be left alone to go about our business."

"And where in our land will this 'business' take place?" El Gato asked harshly.

"Nowhere in your land, hoss. Like I said, we're jist passin' through. I have business to tend to in a place called San Diego, far away by the big water."

El Gato was still suspicious. "Why are you going there?"

Every tribe that Barlow had ever encountered thought the world of their children. The youngsters were treated with respect, dignity, love and much care. He hoped the Apaches were the same.

"My daughter was took by some bad people many moons' ride from here," he said slowly, not wanting to overburden Ortega. "She was only two winters old. That was four, almost five summers ago. I've been lookin' for her ever since. Those bad people left her with White Bear and his people, but some other black-hearted bastards come and took her away from his village."

Barlow paused, letting Ortega catch up. When the Mexican had stopped speaking, El Gato nodded, as if to tell Barlow to continue.

"Me 'n White Bear have been follerin' her trail since then. A winter ago, I learned that some Mexican people had taken her to this San Diego place. I was close to there soon after, but I was ordered by the army back to Santa Fe. I was stuck up there by the winter and the war, still. Then Manuel told me of another way to go, a way that was not cold and snowy." He grinned ruefully. "He didn't, however, tell me it was through the land of the Apache."

El Gato sat in thought, eyes never leaving the white man's. He was still considerably suspicious, but there was the ring of truth in the man's words. Besides, these three had not tried to cause any trouble, had not hunted recklessly, and killed only when attacked.

"You will go in peace," El Gato finally said.

Barlow nodded. *"Muchas gracias,"* he said. He paused, and then asked, "Will other groups of your people hinder us in our travels, hoss?"

El Gato shook his head. "We will send word to our other bands that you are to pass peacefully. Unless you cause trouble with our people," he added in warning.

"Got no plans to, hoss."

16

SEVERAL HOURS LATER, Barlow's small group and the larger Apache group parted on amicable, if not exactly friendly, terms. Each was still rather leery about the other, but they had to trust each other, or else go to war, and neither particularly wanted that.

Barlow and his men packed up their supplies and rode off as quickly as they could manage. They had spent far more time talking with the Apaches than Barlow had wanted to, and had lost valuable traveling time. They pushed it a little harder than usual, trying to make up some of those lost miles, and by the evening, had pretty much done so.

The next day, they slowed their pace to what was normal for them. There had been no sign of Apaches since they had parleyed, not even the uneasy feeling at the back of the neck that Barlow and White Bear had felt before. They relaxed a little.

The land seemed to get more arid with each mile they rode now, and the altitude lower. The days were quite warm, though the temperature still fell considerably at night. There was less vegetation, hardly any real trees anymore, except along the Rio Brave, which was slow moving here. More cactus—and more variations—appeared, along with scrubby grass and plenty of sage.

A few days after the talk with the Apaches, Ortega turned them west, away from the still fairly well-marked road, and away from the river. They moved out into the Sonoran Desert, with its lack of water, brilliant, unblocked sun and its wide-open spaces, which once again had Barlow worrying that they would get lost. There were still some distant mountains to the north and farther to the south to sort of focus on, but that was about all the landmarks they had.

Barlow took to riding fairly close behind Ortega, keeping his eyes focused regularly on the rump of the Mexican's horse. That way he didn't have to look out across the vast wasteland and see nothing but mirages and strange things dancing in the desert heat. It was disconcerting to him, so he avoided it as much as possible.

He had tried closing his eyes as he rode, but that did him no good. For one thing, he too often would fall asleep, and it was annoying to keep jerking awake every few minutes. For another, it blotted out everything but visions of Anna, her mother and her little brother. They moved and talked and called to him in the darkness of his closed eyes. And he could not bear their looks of disappointment and sorrow. It seemed as if Anna was always calling to him, "Where are you, Papa? Why haven't you come for me, Papa?" It was chilling to Barlow, and he had a harder time facing that than he did the open desert.

Two days into the barren land, they made a camp in the middle of the emptiness. There was no cover as far as they could see, no trees or streams, just a few small rocks and some scrubby little sagebrush that might provide shelter. So they just stopped where they were and took care of the animals.

It was still light, though getting near to dusk, and Barlow wandered out a little ways from the camp, wondering if he could figure out where they were in this empty country. As he stood there, Buffalo 2 at his side, a movement caught his eye and he looked down and saw some strange-looking creature slink under a sagebrush. He moved toward the bush, knelt and peered under it. A funny-looking critter, one unlike anything he had seen before, tried to move away from this odd face staring at it, but its movements were slow, almost ponderous for such a small animal.

"Well, hoss, let's jist see what you look like," Barlow muttered. His hand darted forward and grabbed the creature by the tail, and stood, holding the animal at arm's length.

The critter hissed a little, and squiggled, trying to get free. Buffalo 2 bounced around underneath it, trying to figure out what this strange-smelling beast was. The lizard was about a foot and a half long. It had colorful stripes and patches on a dark body, and its stubby little legs flapped impotently.

Barlow headed back toward the camp. As he neared it, he shouted, "Hey, boys, lookee what I got here!"

White Bear looked up and shrugged. When Ortega glanced at Barlow, he froze. "*¡Madre de dios!*" he breathed.

"What's with you, old chap?" White Bear asked.

Ortega didn't bother to answer. He rose and walked slowly toward Barlow, then halted. "Stop, *señor*," he said nervously. When a surprised Barlow did so, the Mexican said, "Turn around and throw that thing as far as you can out into the desert, *amigo!*"

"What fer?" Barlow responded, perplexed. "It's jist some funny-lookin' little critter."

"It is poisonous, *señor*. *Muy* poisonous."

"What, this thing?" Barlow asked, incredulous. He moved closer. "It ain't got fangs or a stinger or nothin'." He swung it back and forth in front of him, smiling. It started to slip from his grasp, and he swept his other hand up to steady it, catching it just behind the short front paws. The creature immediately bit Barlow's arm.

"Goddamn son of a bitch!" Barlow roared as pain shot up his arm. He still had ahold of the tail and yanked it to pull it away from his arm, but it was having nothing to do with that. It had a death grip on Barlow's arm, and seemed to be gnawing on the limb.

Swearing a blue streak in Spanish, Ortega raced up to him, knife in hand. He grabbed the tail from Barlow, lifted it, then severed the lizard in half. He tossed the carcass away. Very carefully, he grabbed the thing's bloody torso and then, with his knife, began to pry open the creature's jaws.

The beast resisted some, but as its life swiftly ebbed, it lost its grip. When it was loose, Ortega flung the thing as far away from camp as he could.

"How're you doing, old chap?" White Bear asked. He had walked up after Ortega did, and had stood at a respectful distance until the Mexican was done.

"I'm jist fine," Barlow growled.

"As I said before, *amigo*," Ortega interjected, "it is poisonous. Very bad."

"I don't feel nothin'," Barlow said. "A little pain where it bit me, that's all. Maybe it didn't git any venom in me."

"We can hope, *señor*," Ortega said skeptically. "But I doubt that's true."

"What the hell is it?" Barlow asked.

"It is called a Gila monster."

"Well, it sure as hell has teeth like a monster. That little bastard really latched on to my arm there."

"*Sí*, that is the way they do it. They don't have fangs like the rattlesnake. They just gnaw on you until they open up your flesh, then the venom flows in from behind the teeth. It is why these things won't let go. They want to make sure they get their poison into you."

"Well, if it did git some in there, I suspect it did a goddamn good job, hoss," Barlow snapped. The pain was becoming intense, and he was a bit queasy. But he would not admit it to the others. "Let go my arm, hoss," he said. When Ortega did so, with a dubious look on his face, Barlow cradled his right arm in his left hand and walked back to the camp, where he plopped down.

"Git me some water, hoss," he said to Ortega as the Mexican and White Bear followed him into the camp.

Ortega brought the gourd and held it up to Barlow's mouth. The former mountain man snatched it out of the Mexican's hand. "I can do it myself, hoss," he snapped. "I ain't helpless." He drank deeply.

Ortega bit back the temper that had begun inside. "You should let me look at that wound, *señor*," he said evenly.

"What in hell fer, hoss?"

"Some people have found out that when the Gila monster bites, it sometimes leaves pieces of their teeth in there. I ought to check to see. If there are, we have to get them out, or the wound could get putrid on you, and we'd have to chop it off." Ortega thought that wasn't all that bad an idea, considering how Barlow was acting at the moment.

"Well, then, goddammit, hoss, go ahead and look at it."

Ortega pulled Barlow's arm toward him none too gently, and shoved the bloody shirtsleeve up. He peered closely. It was nearly dark, but he could still see pretty well.

"Shouldn't you stop the bleeding, old chap?" White Bear asked, leaning over to look for himself.

"Bleeding is good for it, *amigo*. At least for a while. Maybe it will carry some of the poison out." He paused, then said, "I think there are some teeth in there, *señor*. We better take them out."

"Well git to it, you goddamn bean-fartin' son of a bitch," Barlow growled. He had never felt pain this intense. Not even when he had taken that arrow in the chest that got hooked into his breastbone. He was half tempted to cut his own arm off just to stop the pain that throbbed at the site of the bite.

"Before you do that, old chap," White Bear said to Ortega, "I think we need to calm this cantankerous old sod down some." He hurried away and returned with one of their two bottles of whiskey. "Here, old fellow," he said, handing Barlow the bottle, "drink up now like a good lad."

"Now this is the kind of doctorin' that'll do me some good." He took a huge swallow, then swiped his sleeve across his mouth. "You boys want some?" he asked. The other two men shook their heads. "Well, then, all the more for me." He gulped down some more.

By the time he had polished off half a bottle or so, he seemed to be drunk enough for Ortega to begin. He glanced up, shaking his head. Dark was almost upon them, and it was getting difficult to see. He wished they had the materials to make a fire; it would make all this that much more simple. But he couldn't delay. He pulled out his knife and as gingerly as he could, began digging out small pieces of Gila monster teeth.

In ten minutes, he stood, wiping his knife blade on his pants. "I think I got all of them, *señor*," he said to White Bear.

The Shoshoni nodded. He glanced at Barlow, who seemed to be reeling where he sat. "Let's lay him down, *amigo*, before he bloody falls off his seat and cracks that bloomin' thick skull of his."

When that was done, and the whiskey retrieved and replaced in the supplies—after one quick sip for each of the two standees—they sat. They had no fresh meat, so the two dined on jerky and took sparing sips of water.

In the morning, after a repeat repast of the night before, White Bear and Ortega went to check on Barlow. The former mountain man was snoring loudly, but didn't seem to be sleeping all that peacefully. Ortega gently lifted the injured arm, shoved the sleeve back and looked at the wound in the full light of day. It was swollen and looked mighty ugly, with the area around it a variety of sickly colors.

"Think we should wake him, old chap?"

"No, *señor*," Ortega replied. "I think it is best to let him sleep."

"What're we going to do about traveling, mate?" White Bear asked. "We can't stay here long. There's no wood, no water, no game."

"I know, *señor*. But maybe he will wake up soon on his own, then we can be on the move."

White Bear nodded. "You got anything to help him heal?" he asked. "Some poultices or something?"

Ortega shook his head sadly. "I am no *curandaro, se-ñor*," he said quietly. "I have no knowledge of herbs and things. Don't your people use such things?" he asked, looking up at White Bear.

The Shoshoni nodded, but said, "We do, yes, old chap. But I have bloody little knowledge of such things myself. Besides, anything that I'd know how to use wouldn't be available around this bloomin' place." He waved an arm encompassing all they saw. "These bloody plants around here are quite different from those I'm used to."

"Then there is nothing we can do, *amigo*," Ortega said,

pushing to his feet. He looked down sadly at Barlow. "It is in the hands of Jesus Cristo," he added.

"Or the Great Spirit."

"Same thing, I think, *amigo*," Ortega said with a drawn smile. He sighed. "I have heard that these bites are not always fatal. I think it's worse if the infection sets in. *Señor* Barlow is a big, strong man. I think he will come through this all right."

"I hope you're right, Manuel."

Barlow woke in the late morning. He sat up, his face covered with sweat. Then he spun to the side and wretched, losing all the whiskey he had consumed the night before. "Goddamn," he said in surly tones when he was finished, "that was powerful pleasant." He spit, trying to get the last of the foul taste out of his mouth.

"What time is it?" he asked.

"A little before noon, *señor*," Ortega answered after a look at the sun's position.

"I been out a spell, then, ain't I?" Barlow rose to his feet, very awkwardly. He weaved there, and then lurched toward his two friends. "We better git on the trail, boys," he said, the words drawn out, sloppy.

"I think we can afford to stay here for a day, old chap," White Bear said easily. "Let you get over that frightful little bite you have there."

"I don't need no goddamn time to git over it. It ain't nothin' but a small animal bite."

White Bear and Ortega looked dubiously at each other, before the Shoshoni shrugged. "If that's the bloody way you want it, mate, we'll get things ready. You sit and rest a while, until we're bloody finished."

Barlow nodded and sat heavily. He was woozy, and did not like the feeling at all. As he sat there, he lost focus and almost forgot where he was. Everything out in front of him was kind of blurry and indistinct. Only White Bear coming over with a saddled Beelzebub woke him from his stupor.

Barlow rose unsteadily and tried to climb on the mule, but he couldn't muster the strength. "Son of a bitch," he muttered. He slipped his left foot into the stirrup again, and with a mighty effort, managed to pull himself into the saddle. He was bent in half, resting alongside the mule's neck, breathing heavily. He wondered what was going on. He felt as weak as a newborn colt. He tried to push himself up straight in the saddle, but wasn't sure he had accomplished it. He tried to look around, but he was having trouble seeing anything.

"Goddamn, these are some bad doin's," he mumbled, just before falling off Beelzebub and landing in the sand.

"This does not look good, old chap," White Bear said, a touch of worry in his voice.

— 17 —

SHE WAS THERE! His Anna was there! Right in front of him, mere feet away. She recognized him, and called out to him, "Papa! Papa!" over and over. He held out his arms in a welcome embrace, and she ran toward him, happy, laughing, her face joyous. He eagerly prepared for her leap into his powerful arms. He would not let her get away this time.

But she could not reach him. She ran and ran and ran but got no closer to him at all. In fact, it seemed the harder she ran, the farther away from him she got.

The joy dropped from her chubby little girl's face, replaced by terror. "Papa!" she called out, but this time it was in horror and fear instead of joy. "Papa!" It was fainter, hardly loud enough to be heard.

Then she was gone.

"Anna!" Barlow roared, his heart breaking inside his chest. "Anna!"

White Bear and Ortega sat nearby and watched as Barlow moaned and groaned incoherently, and thrashed about on his otter-skin sleeping robe. His face was flushed, sweat beading on his forehead.

Buffalo 2 lay beside him, a look of great concern on his dark, furry face. He whined frequently and often nudged Barlow, as if to wake him from whatever it was that was making his master act so strangely.

"I hope that bloody delirium he's having isn't as bad as it looks, old chap," White Bear said.

"It sounds as if he has found himself in the fires of hell, *señor*," Ortega responded, making the sign of the cross.

It was the next morning, and they were still in the same camping spot. The sun had risen hot and bright, and there they were out in the middle of the godforsaken desert.

"You think we can move him, old chap?"

Ortega pondered that for a while, then shrugged. "I suppose we can, *amigo*. If we can think of a way to do it. I don't think he can get any worse by traveling."

"Want to pull out now, mate?" White Bear asked. "Or should we wait until the morning, and get an earlier start?"

"Let's wait until tomorrow, *amigo*," Ortega said after a bit of thought. "Perhaps he'll come out of the delirium by then. If not, we're no worse off really than we are now. And it will give us time to think of some way we can bring him with us, if he's not capable of riding."

"Have any ideas, old chap?"

Ortega shook his head.

"Do you know of anyplace out in this bloody hellhole that has anything resembling timber? They don't have to be real big trees, but substantial."

"No, *señor*," Ortega said. "Why?"

"If we found some bloody real trees, we could make a bloomin' travois to carry him along," White Bear said in irritation. They had to move on soon—their water was already low.

• • •

If anything, Barlow was worse the next morning. He was sweating profusely, and he alternated between burning up and shivering.

"Damn, old chap, this doesn't look good at all," White Bear observed. He was worried about his friend.

"*Sí, señor,*" Ortega said. There was nothing else he could say. He had no idea if Barlow would ever get better. It certainly didn't seem at the moment as if he would recover. But he had seen people in worse shape survive and go back to being the way they had been, with no lingering ill effects. He thought that if anyone could do it, Will Barlow could.

"Have you come up with any way we might be able to cart the bloody old chap with us, Manuel?"

"I think I might have one idea, *señor*. I don't know if it will work, but . . ." He shrugged.

"Well, old chap, what is it?" White Bear asked impatiently.

"We have several extra blankets. Strong, study ones. I think maybe if we tied two or three of them between two of the pack mules, it would make a litter . . . is that what they call it?"

"Yes," White Bear said with an enthusiastic nod, "that's what it's called. And, by Jove, I think you may be bloody well right, old chap. Let's go give it a try."

It took more than an hour before they were satisfied with the makeshift litter. Getting the blankets to stay in place with any weight on them had been their biggest obstacle, but Ortega, who was well-versed in packing and tying ropes from his days with Antoine Robidoux, finally figured out a way to make it work—by making something like a bedspring out of rope tied to the two pack mules, the blankets could be woven into the ropes in such a way that all would be secure, and none of the ropes would be exposed to cut into Barlow's flesh.

When they finished and stepped back to look at their handiwork, White Bear said, "It doesn't look like much, old chap, but it may get the job done."

"I think we should test it," Ortega said nervously. "I'd hate to put *Señor* Barlow in there and have him go crashing to the ground right away."

Gingerly they approached the makeshift litter from either side. Together they eased themselves up into it, as if climbing into a hammock. The two together weighed considerably more than Barlow and would be a good test. It all seemed to hold, and the two men soon rolled out of the litter.

"Now all we have to do, *amigo*, is to get *Señor* Barlow's big carcass up there," Ortega said, almost smiling.

"That will be difficult, old chap," White Bear agreed.

They led the pack mules to where Barlow lay. Buffalo 2 looked up in confusion. "Go on, Buffalo," White Bear said sternly, "get out of the way."

The dog hesitated, and even growled a little.

"We aren't going to hurt him, old chap," White Bear promised. He knelt and patted the dog's head. "We're just going to put him in this contraption so we can move on and find us some water, and maybe fresh meat."

With the quizzical look still plastered on his face, Buffalo 2 stood and backed up, watching the two men closely.

"Good boy," White Bear said, rising.

He and Ortega bent and hefted Barlow. They were both strong men, but trying to get Barlow's bulk, now little more than dead weight, high enough to slip him into the litter was still a mighty task. They managed, though, and then stood there for a few minutes, puffing hard after the exertion. Within minutes, they were mounted.

"Come on, Buffalo," White Bear called out. He headed

off, towing the rope to the single pack mule as well as Beelzebub. Ortega rode beside him, leading the two pack mules that held Barlow's litter.

He was on a ship of some kind, sailing across vast open waters. Barlow was a little worried about that. This was even more disconcerting than riding across open prairies. But he pushed the concern down. Soon he would be with Anna.

Before long, the ship was edging into a harbor. The city beyond the harbor had a definite Spanish or Mexican look about it, but there were several American flags flying, and more than a few American ships moored there.

As the captain guided the ship into the slip, Barlow leaned over the rail, eyes searching the dock, where dozens of people waited. *There she is,* he realized to his great relief. He waved and shouted, "Anna! Here I am, Anna!"

The little girl looked up and spotted him. She smiled brightly and waved back, excited beyond all measure.

Barlow thought he heard her yell "Papa!", but he couldn't be sure. The ship had docked, and Barlow began bulling his way toward the gangplank, which was just being moved into place. He wanted to be the first one off, but that became impossible as several well-dressed but unmannerly elderly women were there ahead of him. He graciously let them go, then slowly shuffled down the gangplank after them, wishing they would hurry up and move their plump bodies a whole lot faster.

Then he was on the dock and moved a little away from the gangplank. "Anna?" he called. "Anna, I'm here, by the gangplank." He waited anxiously for his daughter to appear. But she did not.

"Anna?" he called again, more frantically. "Anna?"

He pushed through the swirling crowds, shoving people to the side when they didn't move out of his way fast enough. All the while, he called over and over for Anna, his voice growing desperate, his heart racing with anxiety.

A woman screamed, and people turned to look. Soon everyone was streaming toward the other side of the dock. Barlow joined the crowd, and then heard, "It's a child! A child in the water!"

"Goddamn!" he swore silently. He shoved and pushed his way through the mob, not caring about anyone's feelings. He had to get there to make sure it wasn't Anna.

He got to the edge of the dock, and looked down into the water. There was Anna, floating facedown, her fancy little dress billowed out in the water. "No!" he wailed.

Barlow looked around, trying to find someone who could help him, but everyone had backed off, and all were staring at him as if he had suddenly turned into an ogre or a demon of some sort.

He tore off his frock coat and tossed it aside. "I'm comin' for you, Anna," he shouted, then leaped off the dock, hurtling down toward the cold, dark water.

But Anna had vanished. "Anna!" he screamed, the word dragged out in a forlorn plea for help in finding his daughter. "Anna!"

Ortega jerked his horse to a halt, and the pack mules with the litter stopped quickly, too. The Mexican slid out of his saddle and handed his reins to White Bear, who had been only a second or two behind him in stopping. Ortega ran to the litter, and found Barlow coated in sweat but shivering despite the high temperature.

Ortega patted Barlow's forehead and face with an old shirt he had tucked away when they'd left Santa Fe. He had used part of it that morning to make a bandage for Barlow's injured arm. He checked that bandage now. It was still relatively free of blood, and he figured he could leave the bandage alone for the time being.

With a sigh, Ortega got his reins from White Bear. As he did, he said, "More delirium."

Ortega climbed into the saddle and they were off again, both wondering about their friend. "What're we going to do, *señor*," Ortega asked as they rode slowly, "if *Señor* Barlow dies?"

White Bear shrugged. He had never really given it much thought. The idea of Will Barlow ever dying was something that just never entered his mind. He expected the former mountain man to go on forever. Even when they had both been wounded by the Blackfeet, Barlow had been the one to get them going in the right direction to where they could find help. But now that Barlow's death appeared to be a real possibility, he wondered what he would do.

It didn't take the Shoshoni long to find an answer. "I'd go on to bloody San Diego and try to find Anna for him, old chap," he said simply. "It's the least I could do for him. I've met his in-laws, and I'd bring Anna to them as soon as I could."

Ortega nodded. He had expected the Shoshoni to say something like that. He felt the same way himself to a large degree, though he had not known Barlow nearly as long as White Bear had. "Would you let me join you, if it comes to that, *señor*?" he asked quietly.

White Bear glanced over at the Mexican and grinned a little. "I don't see that such a thing would bother me, old chap."

He could see Anna playing in the short grass of the prairie. All thoughts about his dislike for the wide-open spaces were gone. Anna was nearby, and he would be with her in seconds. Nothing could stop him from that now.

"Anna!" he called happily. "Anna, it's your pa!"

The little girl looked up and smiled, its brightness rivaling that of the sun. She turned, holding out the bouquet of wildflowers she had just picked. "For you, Papa!" she called out, and giggled like little girls did.

Barlow's heart sang. After all these years, after all the traveling and searching, she was here and would be in his arms in moments. So many times he had been within reach of her, only to have her slip away at the last moment. But that could not happen this time. She and he were the only people in this vast open land. No one could get in the way of their reunion.

He began to run toward Anna, not wanting to lose another second of her life. But when he was within ten feet of her, a war party of Utes appeared out of nowhere, between him and his daughter. He skidded to a stop, just short of the sharp points of Ute lances. "I want my daughter back, you heathen sons a bitches," he snarled.

"She is ours for the taking, white-eyes," one of the warriors said with a sneer. "You are not a good enough father. You lost her many years ago, now she is gone to you forever."

The warriors turned and raced off, one of them carrying Anna on his horse in front of him. Faintly, her tiny voice came to him, "Papa!"

He started to run again, his thick legs churning. He would run until the end of time, if that's what it took to get her back. "Anna!" he cried out, his breath coming hard in his chest, "Anna!"

But only the prairie wind was there now, carrying his voice to the ends of the earth, but not reaching the only ears that he wanted to hear them.

White Bear and Ortega eased Barlow out of the litter. He seemed to be no better than he had been that morning.

But he didn't seem any worse either. They settled him gently on the ground.

While White Bear went to tend the animals, Ortega changed Barlow's bandage, putting on a fresh piece of cloth. He hoped they came to some water soon, not only because they were low and needed it, but he also wanted to wash the dirty strips of cloth so they could be used as bandages again.

"You may not want this, *señor*," the Mexican whispered, "but I am going to pray to the Holy Mother for you."

He rose and went to help White Bear.

18

BARLOW AWOKE IN strange, but yet familiar, surroundings. His breathing was labored, and his arm hurt like hell. He wasn't sure of what to make of all this. His mind was fuzzy, his memory patchy. He closed his eyes for a few moments and then opened them again, wanting to see if he was still in the same place.

He was, but now there was a beautiful young *señorita* hovering over him. She smiled, and it warmed his heart immediately. "Who are you?" he asked.

"Qué?" she responded.

"Her name's Esperanza," Ortega said, moving into Barlow's field of vision. "Esperanza Lugo."

"It's a beautiful name," Barlow said, letting Ortega translate it for him.

Esperanza smiled sweetly, and left.

"It's about time you were up and about, old chap," White Bear said as he got to the side of the bed. "Manuel and I have gotten considerably tired of doing all the bloody work while you lay there lollygagging about."

"I would've been more'n pleased to have changed

places with you, hoss," Barlow said, his voice still weak and rusty from lack of use.

White Bear smiled. "Do you remember anything at all, old chap?"

Barlow thought for a few moments, then closed his eyes against the pain of remembrance. "I recall dreams about Anna. I was always close enough to reach out and touch her, and then somethin' always interfered. It was poor doin's, hoss, I can tell you that much." He shuddered involuntarily.

"Well, old chap, the fever and delirium seem to have passed, and it appears you'll be right as bloody rain in no time."

Barlow nodded, pleased at the news. "Where'n hell are we?"

"A little Mexican town called Cholla Flats," Ortega answered. "We stumbled on it yesterday. I don't think anybody knows it's here. Including the Apaches. If they haven't attacked here by now, they probably don't know about it."

"That or they see it as harmless for the time being," Barlow said. He bit his lower lip, but had to ask, "How long I been out of my head?"

"A week, perhaps a little more, *señor*," Ortega answered.

"How'd I git here? We was out in the middle of nowhere when that critter latched onto me."

"Manuel here figured out how to make a litter to carry your bloody heavy carcass in, old chap," White Bear said. "We rode on from where that happened and would've kept going until you bloody well woke up or we were in bleedin' San Diego."

"I'm obliged, boys," Barlow said solemnly.

"*De nada,*" Ortega answered for himself and for White Bear. "It was something that had to be done. You would have done the same if it had been either of us."

Barlow nodded. That was a fact, and they all knew it. "So when do we pull out of here? Mornin'?"

"We've had a bloody awful trip while you've been taking your leisure, old chap," the Shoshoni said. "I believe we are due a few days to rest and recover."

"*Sí,*" Ortega tossed in. "It is nice here. Good people, plenty of food, pretty *señoritas.*" He grinned widely.

"Seriously, old chap, you need some more time to recover, and the bloody animals need time to rest up. We've asked a lot of them since we left bloomin' Santa Fe."

Barlow nodded, agreeing. Without the horses and mules, they would die in the desert in no time. "Not too long, though?"

"Couple of days, old chap."

Barlow progressed considerably in those couple of days, that stretched into three, and then four.

On the third night, Esperanza visited Barlow's room well after dark. She slipped through the door and then froze when Buffalo 2 stood and snarled ever so low but fiercely. "*Señor?*" she called nervously. "*Señor* Barlow?"

Barlow had been asleep, but he awoke fast. "Who's there?" he asked.

She didn't really understand, so she just said, "Esperanza," hoping it would be a sufficient answer.

"*Bueno!*" Barlow said. "Buffler, c'mon, now, she's a friend, and you know it."

The dog went and sniffed at the woman, who remained frozen against the door in the darkness. Then the Newfoundland moved off to his corner and plopped down.

Barlow got a couple of decent sized candles going, lighting them from the little one that had been burning on a small side table. "*Aqui,*" Barlow said with a smile, patting the bed.

Esperanza grinned and moved toward the bed, shedding

her clothes as she did. She stopped for a moment at the side of the bed, pleased at the look of desire that had sprung into Barlow's eyes.

Barlow grabbed her wonderfully womanly hips and pulled her into the bed, half on top of him. She giggled, a delightful sound in Barlow's ears. She squiggled around until she was laying flat on top of him. She was thrilled that he was already aroused, his lance pushing up against her womanhood. She spread her legs a little, letting his shaft spring up, then closed her legs, trapping him between her upper thighs. Both moaned in pleasure at the arrangement.

When she smiled at him again, he grinned back, put his hands around the back of her head, and pulled her mouth down to his. The taste of her mouth and lips was wonderful, and he kept them locked together at the lips for a long, long time.

By now, Esperanza's womanly parts were wet and eager for his entrance into her paradise. She pushed herself up, until she was kneeling on her shins, her womanhood hovering above his quivering lance. She grabbed it in a feather-soft hand, making him jump a bit with the delicate but powerful thrill. She eased herself down on him, guiding him into her secret passage.

They rested that way for what seemed a long time, reveling in the pleasure that pulsed through their bodies just from the intimate contact. Then Esperanza began rocking back and forth on him. He reached up and pulled her down a little so his mouth could lovingly attack her breasts.

The combination of her movements and his attentions to her nipples pushed her swiftly to a small, but very rewarding climax. Her shoulders shuddered as it ran its course through her, and then she began her movements again. This time she rode high, where his mouth could not get to her breasts, so his hands replaced his mouth, tantalizing her every bit as much.

Small climaxes came in a steady stream then, until she was shouting, her breath raspy. Finally she said, *"No más. No más, señor."*

His eyes widened in question, but he realized right away that she just needed a few moments break. He gave her as long as she wanted. Then she smiled warmly down on him and began lifting and dropping her hips, allowing his shaft to slide in and out of her pleasure place. Their tempo increased, until she was bouncing frantically atop him, her breasts dancing wildly, exciting Barlow all the more.

His explosion of passion was so powerful that it surprised him. But then Esperanza reached her peak moments later, and he had no more time to concern himself with such mundane matters. He held her bouncing hips firmly in his mighty hands, controlling her enough that she would not pop off him and land on the floor.

Then Esperanza flopped down on his chest, breathing heavily, but smiling in joy. He returned it. Even though his breathing was well behind where it should be, too, her slight frame on his didn't faze him in the least. *"Muchas gracias,"* Barlow said, meaning it. After the Gila monster bite, he wasn't sure he would be able to do anything again. Now he knew this was working well. The rest, he figured, would be fine, too.

When their breathing had returned to normal, Esperanza slipped out of the bed and kissed him lightly on the lips. She tossed on her clothes and slid out the door.

Barlow blew out all but one of the candles, and lay there for a while, letting his body relax. He could still smell her on the bed covers. He smiled into the darkness. "Them was some shinin' doin's," he muttered. He drifted off to sleep.

And the nightmares began again, but not entirely. Instead of the delirium-induced visions he had had before, now there were just snatches of images, shooting before his eyes. A quick flash of Anna's face, and then gone. A stern-looking wife, Sarah, seeming to accuse him of being derelict in his task. A laughing Umpqua braining his son, Will Junior.

He sat up in bed, cursing himself and his visions silently. He stood and paced the room in the dim light of the one flickering, small candle. "Dammit, Anna," he muttered, "I will be there, girl. Soon. I'm comin', girl. You hold on and I'll be there to fetch you home before you know it."

He paced some more. The anger and fear began to melt, and finally he felt he could sleep again. He did, and blissfully this time, waking when a cock crowed somewhere nearby. He rose and dressed, then headed out of the room. It was the first time he had been outside the room since he had been there. He felt good, strong, ready to take on the world and whatever it would throw at him.

He and his two companions sat down to breakfast with Esperanza's family. The food was plentiful and mighty flavorful. Afterward, as the three men were loading their pack mules and saddling their riding animals, Esperanza's father, Jorge, gave the travelers some extra flour and cornmeal, plus some coffee and a bit of sugar.

"Are you sure?" Ortega asked Jorge in Spanish.

"*Sí, sí,*" the father said with a smile beneath his bristly white mustache. Then he left.

"You think that ol' hoss can afford to give us them extry supplies, Manuel?" Barlow asked.

"Probably not, *amigo*. But that is the way of my people sometimes. Generous even if it hurts them."

Barlow nodded. "You boys got any money on you?" he asked.

"A few pesos," White Bear said.

"Same here," Ortega admitted.

"Well, I'm about in the same condition, but I think we ought to give Jorge and his family most of the pesos we got. Their generosity plumb shines with this ol' chil'." A flash of Esperanza's naked body bouncing atop his flickered through his brain, and a shiver of pleasure ran down his spine.

The other two nodded. Barlow gathered up a couple of pesos from his companions, and added some of what he had. All three kept just a few coins in case they would need it later on the trail. He put the money in a small buckskin pouch and then gave it to Ortega, who went to make sure the Lugo family got it, and could not refuse it.

Within minutes, they were riding out of the Lugo family's yard. It was the first time Barlow had seen the town, and he was amazed at how small and run-down it was. That made the Lugo family's generosity even more startling. These people had little of anything except hard times.

In very little time, the town was nothing but a browner splotch against the brown background. "No wonder the Apaches ain't ever raided that place," Barlow said. "It's too goddamn small fer them to find it."

The three laughed.

The journey across the Sonoran Desert was long, and quite tedious, boredom weighing heavy on them. As usual when things got to be this wearisome, Barlow's thoughts turned to Anna and his long quest for her. And, as was usually the case, those thoughts turned dark and gloomy, as he considered the possibility of never finding her. Flashes of the visions he had had in the throes of his delirium would leap into his mind, making him grit his teeth until his jaws ached.

Alleviating the monotony of the travel to some small

degree was the occasional Mexican town they would come across. They would usually spend a night, eating well, and at times, enjoying the comforts of willing *señoritas*. But they never stayed more than one night in any one place. With every mile closer to San Diego they got, the more impatient Barlow became. He would have traveled twenty-four hours a day if his mule could have sustained that pace.

Even though it was only March, the desert was fiery hot during the day, and nearly frigid at night. The men grumbled about that a little, annoyed in knowing they still had several hundred miles to go across the desert.

"I don't know if this shines with me at all, hoss," Barlow said to Ortega one night as the three of them hunkered down against a howling dust storm that threatened to scrape them all down to the bone. "I ain't sure I should've let you talk me into this goddamn venture."

"Why?" Ortega asked, surprised.

"It's been hellacious since the start. Nothin' but troubles all the way. Snowstorms, earthquakes, Apache attacks, bites from poisonous critters, goddamn dust storms that like to tear my skin off. Damn, this sure don't shine with this chil' at all."

"Well, *señor*," Ortega responded defensively, "we could have stayed in Santa Fe. There you would be freezing your *cojones* off, and you'd be riding back and forth between Santa Fe and Taos, delivering useless papers for the *pendejo* soldiers."

"Well, when you put it that way, hoss," Barlow said with a short laugh, "I reckon this ain't so bad after all."

They pushed on the next day, still somewhat awed by the ferocity of the dust storm that had passed through. But despite its power, the storm had not managed to hurt most of the scraggly plants and such in the area. Saguaro cactus still stood proud, their arms aimed at the sky. Mesquite still grew, perhaps a little more gnarly than before, but still there. Sage was still plentiful.

Several weeks after leaving the Lugo family's home, they noted signs that they were approaching the Colorado River.

"I hope them Mohaves ain't as angry as they was last year," Barlow said to both companions.

"That was considerably north of here, old chap," White Bear said, not caring one way or the other.

"That's true, hoss. Mayhap they don't even come this far south. It'd be nice to cross that river without havin' to contend with a bunch of Mohaves out to raise hair, though."

"Bloody well right, old chap," White Bear agreed.

"Are you afraid of the Mohaves?" Ortega asked, surprised. "You've fought Apaches and Blackfeet and many others. I can't believe that you'd be bothered by some Mohaves."

"Hell, no, we ain't afraid of them critters," Barlow said flatly. "Compared to the Apaches and Blackfeet and all them others, these boys're poor excuses for warriors. The trouble is, they're a goddamn nuisance. Sort of like them armadillos," he added with a laugh. "They ain't nothin' to be worried about, but ain't many folks want to mess with 'em."

The others joined in the laughter.

19

THEY WERE PLEASED when they got to the Colorado River and found no Mohaves there. They started making camp, since it was too late in the day to be able to make it across the wide river before dark. Plus the animals needed a rest. They had carried the men and supplies for hundreds and hundreds of miles without complaint or incident. The three travelers decided that the animals deserved a day or two of rest before having to swim across the river, and then cross another couple of hundred miles of desert that was even worse than what they had just come through.

The men, too, wanted a little rest. Even Barlow, who was champing at the bit to get to San Diego and find his daughter, realized the need of some time to regain their strength. It would be good to sit for a day or so and let their muscles relax and stretch after more than a month of traveling.

They were lucky enough to find enough wood for a decent fire, and they had killed an antelope earlier in the day, so they would eat well at least for the night.

Once camp was set up, they put some meat on and coffee, and then Barlow broke out the bottle of whiskey, which he had drunk half of when he had been bitten by the Gila monster. None of the men had taken any more of it, wanting to save it and the one other bottle they had just in case of another emergency. But Barlow figured this was as good a time as any to celebrate getting this far without anyone dying, or even the loss of any animals.

They sat leaning against rocks or saddles, Barlow puffing on his old clay pipe, White Bear and Ortega smoking corn husk cigarettes, passing the bottle around, letting the meat cook. Buffalo 2 lay next to Barlow, asleep, though his ears twitched constantly, keeping track of what was going on around him.

They soon finished the bottle, and Barlow heaved it as hard as he could toward one of the massive volcanic rocks that dotted the area, and was rewarded with a loud crash of shattering glass. They ate and relaxed some more, before turning in shortly after dark had fallen.

The next day, they took their leisure, in between tending the horses and mules, making sure the animals were as fit as they could be, and checking over their equipment and taking stock of their supplies. They napped, too, now and again.

They finally all gathered around the fire, and put the last of the antelope on to cook. They were relaxed and at peace, knowing they didn't have much farther to go. Barlow looked forward to getting Anna back, and being done with this constant traveling. It almost seemed to be really within his grasp now, for the first time since his daughter had been taken.

Suddenly Buffalo 2, who had been lying quietly next to Barlow, jumped up and began barking wildly. He bolted toward a jumble of rocks that had long ago tumbled down from the barren mountain not far behind them. An arrow flew out from behind one of the rocks, barely missing the dog.

"Buffler!" Barlow bellowed. "Git back here, boy."

The dog swung around and darted back toward the fire, two more arrows just missing him.

The three men threw themselves flat on the ground. There was no real cover right here, but from what they had seen, whoever was behind those boulders was not very proficient.

Barlow slid his rifle up, and checked to make sure it was free of dirt and that the cap remained on the nipple. He rested it across his saddle, against which he had been leaning moments ago, and waited.

Ortega was prepared, too, his rifle resting on a small rock. White Bear lay in the dirt, bow in hand, one arrow ready to be nocked, and four others in his left hand.

A few more arrows flew out from behind the rocks, though the attackers did not show themselves at all. Barlow roared as if in pain, as an arrow landed close enough for him to be able to fake an injury. His two companions caught on right away, and with the next couple of volleys of arrows, also pretended to be hit. The three lay there moaning occasionally, sometimes crying out for water. Buffalo 2, laying near Barlow, couldn't figure out what was going on.

Time ticked slowly by, but none of the men moved. Buffalo 2 crept over to his master, and nuzzled him. Barlow paid the dog no mind, staying where he was, unmoving, but able to keep an eye out for movement from behind the boulders.

Finally some Indians began creeping out, heading cautiously toward the travelers. They were Mohaves, Barlow noted with annoyance. They inched forward, bent over to present smaller targets. None of Barlow's men moved; they just continued to wait.

When the Mohaves were less than ten yards away, Barlow jerked his upper torso up a little, grabbed his rifle, which was still lying across the saddle, and fired. A Mohave went down.

At the same time, White Bear surged to his feet, pulling the bowstring back as he did. No sooner was he standing then he let loose with an arrow, followed in quick succession by three more. Two other Mohaves went down and stayed there. Another caught a shaft in his arm. He stopped, turned and then ran for the rocks. White Bear fired the last arrow he had in his hand, and the running Mohave was knocked down on his face. He did not get up.

Ortega fired his rifle moments after Barlow did, in the midst of White Bear's personal flurry of arrows, and knocked a warrior down. He pulled out his pistol, ready to take another shot, but the Mohaves were fleeing. Barlow and White Bear chased after them, tomahawk and war club in hand. They managed to catch two stragglers and dispatch them with little effort.

By now, however, the other Mohaves were gone, well up the trail and perhaps even scattered in the rugged little mountain.

"Think they'll be back, *señor*?" Ortega asked as his two friends returned to the camp.

"I doubt it, hoss," said Barlow flatly. "We put some real deep fear into them boys."

"We better be watchful, though, tonight, old chap," White Bear said. "They might come back with some friends."

"Reckon they might do that," Barlow allowed. "C'mon, hoss," he said to Ortega. "We got us a chore to do."

The three men headed back out into the battlefield. White Bear collected his arrows, cleaned them and put them back in his quiver. Barlow and Ortega grabbed a

Mohave body each and began dragging it to the river. They rolled the corpses into the water and watched for a few seconds as they floated away. Then they went back and got some more. White Bear soon joined them, and before long, they were done with the onerous chore.

Back at the fire, the meat they had been roasting had burned considerably. But they were hungry enough not to care. They whittled away the worst of the burnt spots and chew the rest down hungrily.

Darkness fell soon afterward, and the men turned in after a last batch of coffee. All of them had lived in the wilderness long enough to know that with an enemy possibly lurking nearby, they would sleep away from the fire so as not to be seen. And they moved from where they had been earlier, to further confuse the Mohaves should they actually return.

But morning came without any attack. After they choked down some jerky and finished off the pot of coffee, Barlow rose and said, "You two boys start gittin' them animals loaded."

"Where're you going, old chap?"

"Have me a look-see to find out if them goddamn Mohaves is lurkin' about waitin' to catch us off guard. C'mon, Buffler." He strode off toward the rocks from which the Mohaves had attacked the previous afternoon. No one was there, so he followed the thin trail into the rocky, harsh little mountain. He found no one there either, and no sign that they had come back after fleeing after the short, but bloody skirmish.

Relieved, he and Buffalo 2 headed back to the camp, where Barlow helped his companions in their preparations. Soon they were ready. As he edged his mule toward the water, Barlow had no concerns about Buffalo 2 swimming across the river. The current did not seem strong, and the Newfoundland was a born swimmer. "C'mon,

Buffler," he said, pointing to his right. Still he would make sure the dog was upriver from him. If something happened, Buffalo 2 would simply run into the horses and mules, where he could be rescued.

"You boys ready?" Barlow called, looking back. Both men nodded. He eased Beelzebub into the water. The big mule wasn't sure he liked this idea, but he gamely plunged ahead. The bottom dropped out from under his hooves, and the mule began swimming powerfully, moving rather easily against the steady flow of the water.

To his right by a few feet, Buffalo 2 was paddling strongly, looking like he was enjoying this whole adventure. Barlow smiled. He glanced back.

Ortega was in the water on his horse, and the three pack mules behind him were getting there. White Bear still waited back a little way on shore, alternately watching for trouble with either Barlow or Ortega, and behind him, just in case.

Barlow slapped Beelzebub hard on the rump, and the big, grayish black mule lurched up the bank onto dry ground. He brayed a bit, and Barlow patted the animal's strong neck. "You done good, Beelzebub," he said softly. He slid off the mule and greeted his soaking wet dog, who pranced around happily after his dousing, and then he shook his great coat, flinging water in a wide circle.

Barlow climbed back on Beelzebub and turned to watch his friends' progress. They seemed to be having no trouble. Within minutes, Ortega's horse lurched up the bank, followed by the three pack mules all strung together. The pack animals brayed out their annoyance at this. And then White Bear's war pony was there.

"That weren't so bad," Barlow said with a grin.

"It was bloody troublesome, if you ask me, old chap," White Bear said with mock indignity.

They all laughed, and then turned and headed west. As he had most of the trip, Ortega led the way. Barlow and White Bear alternated riding in the middle towing the pack animals and being at the rear to watch for any trouble that way.

The desert here was different than that which they had crossed before coming to the Colorado River. There was more real sand, blown into dunes. What vegetation was there was small but hardy, with Joshua trees and creosote where there had been saguaros and ocotillos on the east side of the river.

The journey across the Mohave Desert was tough, with little water to be found anywhere. Barlow thought it hard to understand how there could be such a great river here with miles and miles of desert on either side, running right up to the water's edge in most places.

There were, however, dunes and even more of the barren desert mountains to break up the horizon to some degree, which suited Barlow just fine. He had had more than his share of riding in places where there was nothing there but distance.

At least, Barlow thought as they rode, it's not the middle of summer. He figured this place would be hotter than the fires of hell in the summer. As it was, they could move pretty swiftly without taxing the animals too much.

Some nights they were lucky and found a small water hole, even if they had to dig to get any real liquid. But most nights they went dry, trying to save most of the water for the animals.

There were no Mexican settlements out here to make even an occasional night a bit more pleasant, something all the men regretted. A nice bed, a decent meal, and a willing *señorita* would have been mighty welcome. Even the Joshua trees and the hardy creosote bushes had disappeared.

Even worse than the lack of water, Barlow began to think, was the utter boredom. It never seemed to leave. They just plodded along, never seeming to really move, clopping across the sand and hard-packed dirt one monotonous step after another.

With that boredom, arose the thoughts of Anna in Barlow's mind. Sometimes he could manage to keep his thoughts light, picturing himself finding Anna and riding away with her. But mostly, the old horrors returned—thoughts that he would never find his daughter, or that she would not recognize him or want to go with him. The terrible images plagued him with each passing mile.

Eventually, though, they came to the mountain range that they knew separated the desert behind them and the coastal, green region ahead of them. It was only a few days' ride to San Diego once they crossed this mountain range. It, too, was somewhat barren, but the pass through it was nowhere near as tedious and as dangerous as many of the passes Barlow had crossed in the Rocky Mountains. In fact, this mountain range was a piddling thing compared with the grand Rockies.

It still took two days to get through the pass. But on the other side, was something resembling paradise. The vegetation here was lush, as it got plenty of rain from the coast. The precipitation blew eastward from the coast and would get stopped by these mountains, dropping all their moisture on the west side before the empty clouds crossed over to the other side, where they had nothing left to give.

Despite being so relatively close to San Diego, Barlow managed to accept White Bear's suggestion that they spend a day or two here just over the mountain from the desert to give the animals some rest and let them have their fill of grass and water.

Barlow didn't like it, but he knew it was necessary. But now that he was in the vicinity of his destination, he itched to be on the move, to get to San Diego, and to find his daughter. She *was* there, he kept telling himself. She *had* to be.

Still, he did like the time for relaxation. Making it even more pleasant was that they did not have to worry about Indian attacks here. At least he didn't think so. The last time through here, with Kearny's Army of the West, the Indians in these parts had seemed docile enough. Of course, that could've been faked in light of the size of the Army, but Barlow didn't think so. The Indians had had the look of defeat and meekness in their eyes. None had the look of a fierce warrior.

As they pulled out two days later, Barlow felt invigorated from the rest. And from the knowledge that his destination was within reach. He had to keep telling himself to calm down, that he could not run Beelzebub all the way to San Diego. Not without killing the mule. And that would leave him afoot, which meant it would take him twice as long to get to San Diego. So he kept himself and the mule in check, but he occasionally gave his mind free rein to fly the miles to the city and give him some comfort that his quest of many years was about to end.

20

BARLOW LED THE way across the last set of mountains they had to cross. San Diego sat right at the bottom of this coastal range. From the top of the pass, they could see the city spread out below them.

They had come within a mile of the mountains the afternoon before, but night had already fallen, making it too late to go that last mile and then try to cross the range in the dark. So they had camped where they were, Barlow so eager to get to San Diego that he could hardly sleep. He got only snatches of sleep, and was up well before dawn—and long before his two companions. He held out as long as he could, which was hardly any time at all, before waking them and pushing them to hurry along.

White Bear and Ortega had grumbled good-naturedly before picking up the pace of their breakfast and their chores to get ready. They pushed off and rode at a good pace to get to the mountain.

It was still early in the day even as they crested it. The three sat there for a few minutes, savoring the salty air, and the view of the bustling city, which was still Mexican in flavor and nature despite the arrival of the Americans.

The ride down was galling to Barlow, since it had to be made so slowly. The steepness of this hill was treacherous, and even the mules did not like it. Barlow could not help but wish that Kearny had used his army to improve this particular trail.

Then they were on the flat and riding at a nice trot, Barlow's heart pumping wildly in his chest. He and the others stopped beside the first American soldier they saw. Barlow did not know him, despite his time traveling with the Army the summer before.

"Where's General Kearny's headquarters, hoss?" Barlow asked.

"Why do you want to know?" the soldier, a private, asked suspiciously. This was a strange group, he thought, an American who looked like he had been a mountain man at one time, a Mexican and some kind of Indian. Very odd indeed. He was mighty wary of the dog, too. The beast was huge and looked hungry to the soldier.

Barlow was tempted to kick the young man in the teeth, but he knew that would not get him the information he wanted. "I got some dispatches for him. From Colonel Price in Santa Fe."

The private still looked rather dubious, and he stood there scratching his head, trying to decide whether to help these folks or not.

"Look, hoss, I ain't got all day. I got some very important business to tend to soon's I drop them papers off with the general."

The soldier remained doubtful, looking quite perplexed. He wished his sergeant were here. He would know what to do.

"Perhaps he thinks we're going to attack the good general, old chap," White Bear offered.

The soldier's eyes widened in shock and surprise. He

was even more befuddled than before. Finally he shrugged, and explained how to get to the *hacienda* Kearny had commandeered for his headquarters.

"Obliged, hoss," Barlow said only a little sarcastically. He and his friends rode on.

It soon became obvious that either the private had sent them in the wrong direction or was so baffled that he didn't know what he was saying. Barlow could see no sign of Kearny's headquarters. Barlow suspected it was the latter. He spotted another soldier, this one with a corporal's stripe on his sleeve. He hoped he would have better luck this time.

The corporal looked strangely at the group for a few moments when Barlow made his request and explained about the private, then said, "I don't know who that man was, sir," he said without hesitation. "But he must be mad." He swiftly pointed out the way.

Barlow's little group found it with no trouble this time. Barlow pulled the buckskin pouch of dispatches out of his possibles bag. Leaving White Bear and Ortega there with the horses and mules, Barlow headed toward the office, Buffalo 2 at his side.

A soldier stopped him, rifle held diagonally across his chest. "What's your business here, sir?" he asked sternly.

"I got papers from Colonel Price for General Kearny," Barlow answered, his annoyance growing.

"Your name, sir?"

"Will Barlow. He'll know me."

"Yessir. Wait here." The private spun, went through the door, carefully closing it behind him, and then returned a few minutes later. "All right, sir, you can go in. The general's waiting for you. Turn left down the hallway, then straight ahead."

"About goddamn time," Barlow muttered as he shoved past the soldier and into the cool, dim interior of the *ha-*

cienda. Kearny had certainly picked well, Barlow thought, noting the furnishings and knickknacks as he walked through the wide antechamber, then down the foyer.

Kearny was writing, his pen nib scratching noisily across the paper, but Barlow was not in a mood to wait any longer. "You want these damn dispatches, hoss, or don't you?"

Kearny looked up, fire blazing in his eyes. "Is that any way to address a general officer?" he asked harshly.

Barlow shrugged. "It is when that general officer acts like an ass," he said evenly.

"I'll have you flogged until you're on your deathbed," Kearny shouted, rising and placing his hands on the desk. "The effrontery of such . . ."

"Take it easy, hoss, before you rupture somethin' inside," Barlow said flatly.

Kearny sputtered some, but sat.

"Look, hoss," Barlow said with a sigh, "you know me and you know how I am. You also ought to remember why I tried to git to San Diego in the first place. But you, you son of a bitch, sent me back to Taos and Santa Fe when I was just a few miles from findin' my daughter." He paused to get himself in check. His anger was pushing up from his chest and beginning to boil out with his words.

"I can't keep track of such things for everyone," Kearny said unapologetically.

"Goddammit, hoss," Barlow snapped, "how many men you had working for you is built like me and has a goddamn great big black dog with him? I don't know what's got your feathers all ruffled, but I ain't about to take such slights as you've tried to give me."

He paused again. "Here are the dispatches from Colonel Price," he finally said, tossing the package on the general's desk. "And as of this moment, I am done with service to you and your goddamn Army, hoss. Me'n White Bear both've had enough of you and your nonsense, and we hereby officially resign. However, you do owe me a heap of pesos for carryin' that packet to you."

"Like hell," Kearny snarled. "You were coming out here anyway."

"I reckon that's true, hoss. But I could've tossed that pouch out in the mountains or in the desert, or in the Colorado when I crossed it. There was nothin' to make me deliver it, 'cept my word, which I gave to Colonel Price, though not directly. Still, my word is worth somethin', hoss. I ain't so sure yours is."

Kearny looked ready to burst from anger, but he managed to get himself under control. The political situation here was not of Barlow's doing, he told himself, and he should not be taking his frustrations out on this man. He finally nodded. "Very well, Mister Barlow," he said tightly, though with less rage. "Since I have been in control of California for more than half a year now, I can see no more need for the services of you and that damned Indian friend of yours." He scratched something on a piece of paper and held it out for Barlow. "A voucher for some pay for the two of you. Probably more than you really deserve, mister, but it'll get you out of my hair once and for all, I hope. Take it to the paymaster. He's headquartered three houses down the street, that way." He pointed.

Barlow took the paper, glanced at it, contained his surprise, and nodded. "Obliged, General." He turned and headed out of the room, and out of the *hacienda*. He took the few minutes to stop at the paymaster's, again leaving White Bear and Ortega outside. When he came out, he split the coins with White Bear, then said, "We best find a place to stay, fill our meatbags, and then start our search."

Two hours later, they had three rooms in a boarding-house run by a spry elderly Mexican woman, and had eaten their fill in a cantina, served by two delightful-look-ing *señoritas*. But Barlow's mind was not on women now; just one tiny female.

The three men and the dog stopped just outside the cantina. "Where do we start, *amigo*?" Ortega asked.

"Hell if I know," Barlow said, suddenly uneasy. He had half expected to ride into this city and see Anna sitting there waiting for him. Even though he had known that was lunacy, he had never really considered the realities of looking for his daughter once he got here.

"That's not much help, *señor*," Ortega said cautiously. He knew Barlow's volatile temper quite well, and he knew that the big man was struggling with his quest right now. He didn't want to anger him.

"Hold on, there, hoss," Barlow suddenly said. "We got a name. Natividad found out the name of the family who has Anna." He had forgotten all about it until now, even though the name was burned into his memory. "It was Morales." He had the sudden sickening realization that he wasn't at all certain that the name Natividad had squeezed out of someone was really the right one.

Ortega nodded. "It's not much, *amigo*, but it is a place to start. That's better than nothing, eh?" He stepped in front of a Mexican man walking past the cantina. *"Por favor,"* he said with a pleasant smile. Then he spoke a few sentences in Spanish.

The man responded and pointed several time in various directions.

Ortega nodded and moved out of the man's way to let him pass, then said to Barlow, "I asked him if he knew where the Morales family lived. He says there are many

Morales families here. It is a common name, *amigo*," he added apologetically.

Barlow nodded. "It still gives us somethin' to begin with, hoss," he said quietly. "All we have to do is start looking for families named Morales. It ain't great, but it's better'n not havin' any name at all."

"*Sí*. The man, he says he knows a couple of Moraleses, and he pointed out where to find them."

"Then let's go, hoss. Time's a-wastin'."

As they had done when they first arrived in Taos and Santa Fe, Barlow, White Bear and Ortega went from house to house asking if anyone there knew anything of Anna. The major difference is that they stopped only at houses with people named Morales. And at each one, they asked if that family knew of any other families with the same name. That kept them going.

They met far less resistance in San Diego than they had in Santa Fe and Taos, at least in most cases. There was an undercurrent of resentment in many of the people, due to the Americans having taken over the city and everything else for miles around, but there was no overt hostility.

As the days dragged by with no luck, the melancholy began to settle in on Barlow again. He was becoming certain that he would not find Anna; sure that whoever had told Natividad that a family named Morales had his daughter had been lying. He was frustrated, worried and in poor humors.

Then one day, nearly two weeks after they had arrived in San Diego, they were in a house when Ortega asked his question. The man of the house, Silvio Morales, froze, not saying anything.

Ortega looked at Barlow, his eyes wide. Looking back at Morales, he let loose a torrent of Spanish, much of it angry.

Morales shook his head, and answered in his own language. He looked frightened, though.

"He says he knows nothing of such a girl," Ortega finally told Barlow.

"And I think he's a lyin' son of a bitch," Barlow snapped heatedly. He paused to calm down a bit. "I ain't sure whether he's got Anna or if he jist knows where she is, but he ain't tellin' true when he says he don't know nothin'."

He stopped, thinking. Then said, "Tell him I don't hate him and I ain't gonna hurt him. Tell him I jist want my daughter back is all. I don't much care how he got her, or how anyone got her, if it's some other Morales family. That don't matter to me. I jist want Anna back."

Ortega translated, then listened. He looked back at Barlow. "He still says he knows nothing, *amigo*."

Killing Morales, which is what Barlow wanted to do, would not solve anything, and it would not get him any answers. He sighed, frustration—and rage—building inside of him like lava in a volcano. He was about ready to burst. Finally Barlow rose, shouting, "Tell him I'll be back, hoss," as he stomped out of the Morales home.

After an hour of aimless wandering around the streets of San Diego, trying to figure out how to get the answers he needed without any bloodshed, he returned to his room. He had no solution, infuriating him all the more.

White Bear and Ortega had heard him arrive, and they went to Barlow's room. Seeing the state he was in, White Bear said, "You better stay here for a while, old chap."

Barlow said nothing, just looked daggers at his friend.

White Bear and Ortega left, and encountered the three Mexican women they had met shortly after arriving in San Diego. "This is no time to be around us, *señoritas*," Ortega said in Spanish. He explained a little about what was going on, and sent them on their way, telling him they would find them when things were settled.

Over the next two days, while Barlow sat in his room stewing with growing anger at being so close to Anna but yet seemingly still so far away, Ortega spent his time asking more questions. Without the glowering Barlow and the hard-looking White Bear, he found that the townspeople were more willing to open up.

Two days later, early in the afternoon, Ortega shoved into Barlow's room.

"Git out, hoss," Barlow growled.

"I found out from some of his neighbors that Silvio Morales does, indeed, have a 'daughter' that could very well be Anna."

Barlow looked up, eyes burning with rage. "That true, hoss?" he asked harshly.

"I can't be sure, of course, *amigo*," Ortega said. "But his neighbors say this little girl looks like the girl you described to me."

"C'mon, Buffler," Barlow roared, charging out of the room with the dog right behind him. Ortega and White Bear hurried to catch up to their friend.

Barlow charged straight to the Silvio Morales residence. Mashing down the front door with his great strength, he thundered inside. Grabbing Morales by the throat and lifting him off the ground, Barlow growled, and Ortega frantically translated, "Git my little girl out here now, hoss, or I'll tear you into tiny pieces, you son of a bitch, and then go find her myself. And if I gotta do that, there's no telling who else in your family will git hurt."

Morales gulped, which was hard to do with Barlow's massive hands on his throat. He said something in Spanish, the words cracked and broken with the pressure on his neck.

"He says he can't call her with you choking him like that," Ortega translated. "Let him down."

Barlow glowered at Morales for a moment, then set him on his feet and released his throat.

Morales rubbed his neck and then called out to someone. Moments later, a woman entered the room with a well-dressed, freshly scrubbed girl of six or so.

Barlow's emotions were raging. For so long he had waited for this moment. Now that it was here, he was almost in shock. He shook his head to clear the cobwebs, knelt and asked, with Ortega continuing to translate, "Do you know me, *señorita*?"

The girl shook her head shyly.

"I'm your father. You was took from me a long time ago, when you were jist a wee thing. I've been lookin' for you ever since. Now I'm here to take you home."

Anna burst into tears, and blubbered in Spanish.

"She says her name is not Anna. It's Raquel. And she says she does not want to leave her 'home,' *amigo*," Ortega explained.

After five years of searching for her, Barlow did not want to hear such a thing. He figured she would be fine once he got her back to the Willamette Valley living with him, as well as her grandparents.

"Go git your things, Anna, and come with me," he said firmly.

Seeing the girl's misery, White Bear grabbed the shoulder of Barlow's shirt and tugged him up. "You can't take her now, old chap," he said quietly. "Let her have some time to get used to this idea. She's only a child and doesn't understand. You've looked for her for five years, mate. You know where she is now, and a few more bloody days away from her to let her get used to you again won't hurt."

Barlow turned angry eyes on the Shoshoni, who stared

calmly back at him. "Damn!" Barlow snapped. "All right." He turned to Morales. "I'll be back often, hoss. If you send her away or try to hide her again, I will make wolf bait out of you and your whole goddamn family."

Without waiting for Ortega to finish translating, he stomped out.

Over the next several days, Barlow spent a considerable amount of time with Anna, trying to let her get used to him and what he was to her. In visiting the house so much, with Ortega translating, he did learn that the Morales family considered Anna a daughter, not a slave. They had thought she was Mexican, not part Indian, and had treated her well. They also said they would continue to treat her as one of the family, if Barlow would let her stay.

That didn't help Barlow's humor any. He almost wished that they had treated her poorly. Then she wouldn't be so reluctant to leave with him. Of course, he did not want her to ever suffer, so that wish was only halfhearted.

Despite Barlow's visits, Anna remained resistant to his overtures.

One night in their rooms, Barlow paced for a long while. Then he ranted, "Tomorrow. Tomorrow we leave here. And Anna's going with me. Ain't nobody gonna stop me neither." He quit pacing and glared from White Bear to Ortega.

"The best thing for that girl, old chap, is for her to stay right where she is," White Bear said evenly.

Barlow went berserk. He grabbed his Shoshoni friend by the shirt, hoisted him a little and slammed his back against the wall. "Don't ever say anythin' that goddamn odious to me again, hoss," he raged. "You do, and I'll kill you."

"Put me down, old chap," White Bear said calmly. "Or

Manuel over there might have to shoot you."

"He does and Buffler'll git him."

"Probably, mate, but you won't be around to know about it."

Barlow reluctantly released White Bear and turned hate-filled eyes on Ortega.

"To take her from the Morales family," White Bear said, "would be just as bad as the bloody Umpquas having taken her from you in the first place."

"You're mad," Barlow growled.

"Am I, old chap? She doesn't know you any more than she does me. She's been with this family more than a year, and they have treated her well. Anyone can see that. To tear her away from that would be cruel to the child, my friend."

"You ain't making no sense," Barlow snapped not very convincingly.

"Do you love this child, old chap?"

"She's everything to me, hoss. You know that."

"Then leave her with the Morales family. That would show your bloody love more than anything else you could do, old chap."

Barlow very slowly started to realize that what White Bear was saying was true. Not only did Anna no longer know him, she probably never would, and she likely would resent him for taking her away from the only family she had ever really known.

Brokenhearted, Barlow sat on his bed. "Goddamn, hoss," he said, close to tears, "you are one goddamn evil critter when you're right. Dammit." Shaking his head at the pain in his chest, he said, "I reckon you are right, hoss. Leavin' her here'd be best for her."

He had a fitful night, full of dreams and nightmares and terrors, all revolving around Anna and his losing her again after all this time. In the morning, though, he paid Anna one last visit.

"I'm goin' away, Anna," he said quietly, kneeling before her again. "The Moraleses are your family now."

Her face brightened after Ortega had translated that.

"But I did want to give you somethin' before I go." He pulled a small, beautifully beaded buckskin pouch from under his shirt and held it out to her. "This was your ma's," he said, choking back tears. "Her name was Sarah."

Anna, who had continued to insist that her name was Raquel, took the pouch reverently. "It's pretty," she said in Spanish. Barlow didn't need that translated. He leaned forward and kissed the girl lightly on the cheek.

Barlow rose and glared with angry, tear-filled eyes at Silvio Morales. "You best treat my little Anna well, hoss," he said, voice thick with sadness. "Or I'll be back." He left the house, a concerned Buffalo 2 at his side, his two friends following him.

He went straight to his room and packed his few belongings. Then he went out back and saddled Beelzebub. White Bear did the same.

As they were finishing, Ortega came up. "Do you mind, *señor*," he asked tentatively, "if I stay here?"

"Got somethin' going with that little *señorita*, eh?" Barlow said, trying for levity but failing miserably.

"*Sí*."

Barlow turned and shook Ortega's hand. "You've been a big help, hoss," he said. "I wish you well." He pulled himself into the saddle. "Ready, hoss?" he asked White Bear.

"Indeed, old chap."

Bearing the crushing weight of his sadness, Barlow rode out of town, accompanied by White Bear and Buffalo 2. Barlow had no idea of where to go or what he would do with his life. He simply had to get away from San Diego. The knowledge that the loss of his daughter would sit in his heart forever was almost crushing him, and he could not stay so close to her and not be with her.

At the crest of the mountain, Barlow stopped and turned to face the city below. "Good-bye, my dear Anna," he said, unashamed of the tears that rolled down his weathered face. He turned the mule and rode off, great shoulders slumped, head bowed.

JAKE LOGAN
TODAY'S HOTTEST ACTION WESTERN!